*What do.*

Christine Christian **has always used her head.**

And it's always paid off for her, big time. Her career as an on-camera journalist has hit a sweet spot. She has the attention of her network, a loyal following of fans who find her long-form feature reports fair, comprehensive, and riveting. Even her love life was finally looking up, with the hot focus and sometimes tender attentions of wealthy, mature bachelor Joseph Calvin.

But lately, when it's her turn to drive down to Santa Barbara for the night, he suddenly has to leave town for an unexpected meeting. When he makes time to drive to Santa Maria for their makeup tryst, she has to fly out at the last minute for her next assignment. Their dating history is a list of rain checks, and these days, the rain never lets up.

Christine **has always been slightly obsessed.**

The hardest thing for her to do is put a story to bed. Consequently, she pulls a lot of all-nighters. And when a lead comes through, she throws everything else to the wind, including caution. She prides herself on following her gut instinct, sniffing out a story where other reporters give up. But when that sixth sense offers a warning, she tends to use her over-smart head to suppress the danger, ignoring her intuition.

Milford-Haven **is a little town up the coast that promised the biggest story of her career so far.**

So she drives there in the dead of night, keeping Joseph waiting for their latest makeup date, and ignoring both common courtesy, and the prickly sense that something is wrong.

Now she faces the most complex, beguiling, and downright confusing puzzle she'll ever have to face. Did the terrifying out-of-body experience she keeps reliving really happen? Why is she suffering memory loss only about certain things? Why does the Central Coast law enforcement officer look familiar?

She takes a nasty fall at the unfinished house where she's agreed to meet her contact, and gets a head injury. She has the lump to prove it. That explains some of the memory lapses. But is it actually worse than that? Has Chris lost her mind? No matter how logically she tries to think through her current dilemma, nothing seems to make sense. Some untapped, inner sense keeps telling her something larger is happening, and there's more at stake than the story, or even her own sanity. Can she learn to hear that inner message before it's too late?

Come discover what happens in . . . ***What the Soul Suspects.***

THE PRESS PRAISES MARA PURL'S
MILFORD-HAVEN NOVELS
What the Soul Suspects

"Mara Purl is a master at drawing you into a story and keeping you in it until the very last page. Even though *What the Soul Suspects* is not like her previous books, she does keep her setting as the Central California coast, and she does bring in some of the characters from past books. This one features Christine Christian, and takes us back to a previous book, *What The Heart Knows*. where we were first introduced to her. If you follow the Milford Haven series, we don't read about Christine again until now. In *What the Soul Suspects*, we do experience quite a bit of the paranormal, in that Christine is prominently featured but as we quickly learn, it's her ghost, or soul, we're reading about. This book was entertaining but in a disturbing way, and it delved much deeper into the human psyche than Purl's previous books. I'm eager to learn if investigator Delmar Johnson will ever know what happened to Christine. Stay tuned..."

– Linda Thompson, Host of *TheAuthorsShow.com*

What the Soul Suspects COMMENTS FROM READERS

"I LOVE this book! Spooky stuff told in a very provocative way . . . with wisdom! It's a wonderful book, so rich and nuanced with exploration of time, space, mind-states and special sensitivities. Much as I've enjoyed Mara Purl's writing in the past, there's something really special about this book that sparkles with conviction, mystery and beauty. There is something so elegant and inviting in this prose . . . really magical! It's not just the substance of the story but also the way it's being told. We're really there with Chris . . . as she drives through the Central Coast. I'm swept up into her world. It captivated me!"

– Marilyn Harris, Singer, Songwriter, Composer

"Cool ghost story with two compelling characters, lots of real-world and metaphysical intrigue and even a dose of Laura Nyro. What's not to like! I found the prose style to be precise and painstakingly visual. The overall atmosphere of the narrative, almost a third major character, also comes to life effectively, as do the lighthouses and spiritual Native American influences, and the notion, at the end, of Chris actually teaming up with Del from the Afterlife to catch her murderer is quite provocative. Purl's imagination and craft keep getting better and better."

– Mark Kudlow, screenwriter

"The voices and personalities are clear and well crafted. The plot unfolds with just the right amount of mystery and strangeness, but never too bizarre as to be unbelieveable. I was yearning for more...thus showing me that it was very compelling from beginning to end. I kept thinking 'great insight', 'very wise', or 'aha!' as I read. I love learning new things in a story!"

– Laurie Jameson, WILLA Award-winning author

"The book is so intriguing and very good! It was so fun to read about an area that I actually lived in. I think you described it beautifully and I felt as if I was there once again."

– Antoinette Burns

THE PRESS PRAISES MARA PURL'S
MILFORD-HAVEN NOVELS

Novel One – *What the Heart Knows*

"Former *Days of Our Lives* star Purl presents the first novel in her Milford-Haven series, which . . . features a setting of unadulterated beauty—the small coastal town of Milford-Haven, CA in the prosperous mid-'90s—and a cast of successful, sexy, sometimes quirkily independent characters. . . . Readers will find details galore . . . and the novel's many inner monologues reveal scheming, secretly confused, or flawed personalities. . . . Milford-Haven offers depictions of daily life, hints of possible future romance, the threat of scandal, and carefully parsed out mystery. . . . the novel is poised to convince readers to continue with the series."

– Publishers Weekly

"Former *Days of Our Lives* actress Purl imbues her soap opera finesse into the fictional setting of Milford-Haven, a sleepy California coastal town. This may be Apple Pie, USA, but hearts are on the line, professions are at stake and a possible murder has tainted the landscape. A whirlwind of juicy drama with dangling-carrot closure."

– Kirkus Review

"*What the Heart Knows* is an upbeat novel . . . the first book of Milford-Haven. The book opens powerfully . . . Purl does not use external paraphernalia to bring her characters to life. Multiple love stories, friendships, crushes. . . . Purl's characters are well-traveled, educated, and street smart."

– ForeWord Magazine

". . . in Mara Purl's enchanting novel *What the Heart Knows* . . . although the picturesque, seaside setting of Milford-Haven plays an important role in the novel, the cast of interesting and eccentric characters is what really draws the reader into the book."

– BookWire

"Mara Purl's *What the Heart Knows* is a first class novel by a very talented writer with strong believable characters, a rapid pace delivery of story, and very tight writing that make this novel such a delight to read. I look forward to seeing other titles in this impressive series."

– Gary Roen, Nationally Syndicated Bookreviewer

Novel Two – *Where the Heart Lives*

In *Where the Heart Lives,* Mara Purl strategically presents a glamorous alternative to big city vibrancy. In the second installment of her already popular Milford-Haven series, the California Central Coast is once again the locale for her magnetic cast of characters. Purl's success is based on her ability to appeal to readers on a more elevated level than traditional romance fiction generally prescribes. Though she never loses the common touch in her storytelling instincts, in every potential stereotype emerges a well-developed character with a standout personality.

— ForeWord Reviews

"[In] the second volume of this ongoing saga . . . Purl returns to picturesque Milford-Haven. The town is filled with back stories—dark secrets, hidden agendas, failed romances and budding love, not to mention the unsolved mystery. Skillfully interspersing the moment-to-moment thoughts of her characters with their actions and dialogue, Purl effortlessly moves from one personal story to another. Like visiting friends and catching up. . . ."

– Kirkus Review

"Part small-town confidential, part mystery, part romance, the story is cozy in the best sense of the word. Steeped in California charm, the setting plays host to a wide variety of characters from across the social spectrum. High society rubs shoulders with artists and diner cooks, providing a snap shot of an up-scale village. Despite the town's air of quaint charm, the people are refreshingly realistic."

– Bookwire

"[In] the second Milford-Haven novel, award-winning writer Mara Purl deepens the intrigue in this captivating window into the little battles, victories, successes, and failings of ordinary people in [the] complicated world [of] Milford-Haven."

– Midwest Book Review

The *Milford-Haven* Series

"In Mara Purl's books the writing is crisp and clean, the dialogue realistic, the scenes well described. I salute her ingenuity."

– Bob Johnson, Former Managing Editor
The Associated Press

"Every reader who enjoys book series about small town life has a treat to anticipate in . . . Mara Purl's *Milford-Haven Novels*."

– Dee Ann Ray, The Clinton Daily News

"Mara Purl's characters have become old friends and I keep expecting one of them to give me a call!"

– Nanci Cone, Ventura Breeze

". . . an intrigu[ing] cast of diverse characters."

– Fred Klein, Santa Barbara News Press

"You can't escape the pull of Milford-Haven, the setting for *Days of Our Lives* actress and award-winning author Mara Purl's enticing new novel *What the Heart Knows*. My kind of romance, this [is a] juicy, read . . . plus, the inviting story makes you think."

– Charlotte Hill, Boomer Brief

"I read Mara Purl's *What the Heart Knows* and loved the book—just devoured it, in fact—and can't wait to read the next installment."

– Anne L. Holmes, APR
National Association of Baby Boomer Women

ENDORSEMENTS FROM OTHER AUTHORS

"Mara Purl is a skillful storyteller who has written a charming and tantalizing saga about the ways in which lives can intersect and be forever changed. The first novel in the saga is not-to-be-missed."

– Margaret Coel
New York Times Best-Selling author
of the Wind River series

"I found a kinship with . . . your heart for character . . . and with your truly fine unveiling of story events."

– Jane Kirkpatrick, Author
Wrangler Award, Willa Award

"I so admire Mara Purl's writing style. The pictures she paints are just glorious, her characters and attention to detail inspiring."

– Sheri Anderson
Emmy Award-winning writer, Days of Our Lives
Author, Salem Secrets Series

What the
Soul
Suspects

Also by MARA PURL

Fiction

When the Heart Listens:
A Milford-Haven Novella

When Hummers Dream:
A Milford-Haven Novelette

When Whales Watch:
A Milford-Haven Novella

When Otters Play:
A Milford-Haven Novella

What the Heart Knows:
A Milford-Haven Novel (Book One)

Where the Heart Lives:
A Milford-Haven Novel (Book Two)

Where an Angel's On a Rope:
A Milford-Haven Holiday Novelette

When Angels Paint:
A Milford-Haven Holiday Novelette

Whose Angel Key Ring:
A Milford-Haven Holiday Novella

Christmas Angels:
A Milford-Haven Story Collection

The Milford-Haven Novels:
Early Editions

Non-Fiction

Act Right:
A Manual for the On-Camera Actor
(with Erin Gray)

Kenneth Leventhal & Co.:
A History of the Firm

S.T.A.R –Student Theatre & Radio
High School Curriculum; College Curriculum

Plays	**Radio Plays**	**S.T.A.R.** **Radio Plays**
Mary Shelley– *In Her Own Words* (with Sydney Swire)	*Milford-Haven, U.S.A* (100 episodes)	*America the Beautiful* *Ashton Valley*
Dracula's Last Tour	*Green Valley*	*Boom* *Caught in a Web*
	Haven Ten	*Changes*
Screenplays & **Teleplays**	**S.T.A.R.** **Teleplay**	*Cruising* *The Curse of* *Santa Florida*
The Meridian Factor (with Verne Nobles)	*Only A Test*	*Deep Freeze* *Fountain Hills Mall*
Welcome to *Milford-Haven* (with Katherine Doughtie Nolan)		*Friendz* *Frozen Hearts* *The Game* *Going Somewhere*
Guiding Light		*In or Out* *The Journal* *K-RAP* *Love Child* *Love Resolutions* *The New Girl* *The Peak Mystery* *San Feliz* *Secretos* *Tokyo Time Travel* *Toxicity* *Westland High* *Wrong Way*

Mara Purl

What the Soul Suspects

A Milford-Haven Paranormal Novella

Bellekeep
Books

What the Soul Suspects © 2020

Milford-Haven
PUBLISHING, RECORDING & BROADCASTING HISTORY
This book is based upon the original radio drama Milford-Haven ©1987 by
Mara Purl, Library of Congress numbers SR188828, SR190790, SR194010;
and upon the original radio drama Milford-Haven, U.S.A. ©1992 by Mara Purl,
Library of Congress number SR232-483, broadcast by the British Broadcasting
Company's BBC Radio 5 Network, and which is also currently in release
in audio formats as Milford-Haven, U.S.A. ©1992 by Mara Purl.
Portions of this material may also appear on the
Milford-Haven Web Site, www.MilfordHaven.com or on
www.MaraPurl.com
© by Mara Purl. All rights reserved.
No part of this book may be reproduced or transmitted in any form or by
any means, electronic or mechanical, including photocopying, recording, or
by any information storage and retrieval system, without permission in
writing from the publisher. For information address: Bellekeep Books
29 Fifth Avenue, Suite 7A, New York, NY 10003
www.BellekeepBooks.com
Front Cover – Original Watercolor by Mary Helsaple ©2019
Front Cover design by Reya Patton, Nick Zelinger, and Rebecca Finkel
©2019 by Milford-Haven Enterprises, LLC.
Copy Editor: Laurie Jameson. Proofreader Todd Andrews.
Typesetter & Layout: Rebecca Finkel
Author photo: Ashlee Bratton

Publisher's Cataloging-In-Publication Data
Names: Purl, Mara, author.
Title: What the soul suspects / Mara Purl.
Other Titles: Milford-Haven U.S.A. (Radio program)
Milford-Haven (Radio program)
Description: New York, NY : Bellekeep Books, [2020]
Series: A Milford-Haven novella | Based upon the original radio dramas
Milford-Haven and Milford-Haven U.S.A., broadcast by BBC Radio 5 Network.
Identifiers:
ISBN 9781936878987
ISBN 9781936878482 (ebook)
Subjects: LCSH: Women journalists—California—Fiction.
Astral projection—Fiction. | Murder—Investigation—California—Fiction.
Death—Fiction. | California—Fiction. | LCGFT: Paranormal fiction.
Classification:
LCC PS3566.U75 W452 2020 (print)
LCC PS3566.U75 (ebook)
DDC 813/.6—dc23

Published in print edition in the U.S. by Bellekeep Books, New York www.BellekeepBooks.com.
Published in audio in the U.S. by Haven Books, Los Angeles www.HavenBooks.net

10 9 8 7 6 5 4 3 2 1

Printed in the United States of America

*This book is dedicated to
my mother
Marshelline Patton Purl
whose spirit lives on,
and who always believed
Chris Christian never died.*

Acknowledgments

Thanks to my publishers: Patrice Samara, Kara Johnson and Tara Goff at Bellekeep for vision, guidance and faith. Thanks to my gifted editorial team: Vicki Hessel Werkley, editor; Laurie Jameson, editor; Rebecca Finkel layout designer. Thanks to my talented book cover team: Mary Helsaple for exquisite watercolors, Tara Goff for design concept, Kevin Meyer, Nick Zelinger and Rebecca Finkel for beautiful, evolving layout. Thanks to my marketing team: Jonatha King at King Communications for PR and marketing; Kelly Johnson for Internet and social media wizardry; Sky Esser and Amber Ludwig for web design. And thanks to Judith Briles for marketing wisdom.

Thanks to those who provide expertise during my research: for "Miranda," to artists Mary Helsaple and Caren Pearson for inspiration and depth of detail; to Reid Miller, Associated Press, for mentoring and friendship. Thanks to Pilulaw Khus for Chumash wisdom; and to the Chumash Wishtoyo Foundation for beautiful programs and Ted-X presentations. For lighthouse history and operational details, thanks to: Carole Adams and Harrison Gruman at Piedras Blancas lighthouse; Kim Castroban at Point Vicente lighthouse; Deborah Foughty at Point San Luis lighthouse.

Musical artists mentioned: Grammy winner Keb Mo (find his music and tour dates at KebMo.com); the late Jim Bartow's music, performing and teaching included with his permission, and with thanks for his mentorship and friendship for many years; the late Jim Morrison, rock icon and poet; the late Laura Nyro and our mutual friend Felix Cavaliere for that connection, and Rashid Silvera for dropping the needle.

Thanks to dear friends in the Central Coast who've supported Milford-Haven for many years with such enthusiasm, including Elaine Evans, Kathe Tanner, Susan Berry, Judy Salamacha, Linda Wilson, Carol Schmidt and Dennis Eamon Young. And to my colleagues at the Central Coast chapter of Sisters in Crime, the members of SLO Night writers, and colleagues at the Central Coast Writers Conference and the Writers in Action Conference.

Thanks to Verne Nobles, Frank Abatemarco and Patrice Samara for vision and commitment to the Milford-Haven Television project.

Thanks to sponsors and co-hosts past and future for helping me produce the Milford-Haven Chari-Tea® Events (Possibili-Teas, Generosi-Teas, Hospitali-Teas, Creativi-Teas, Connective-Teas, and our list continues!)

The first versions of these books were novelizations—adaptations of scripts into a fledgling narrative version. One person who "got" what I was doing, even then, was my mentor Louis L'Amour, who believed in my project and told me to keep going with it. For encouragement and friendship my forever thanks to Louis, to Kathy L'Amour, Beau L'Amour and Angelique L'Amour Pitney. The other two people who always got it were my parents. Thanks to Pre who introduced me to Shakespeare and to Dickens. Thanks to Mom who always believed I should be writing and who helped me create the first Tea events.

And most important of all—thanks to you, my readers! I'm thrilled to welcome those of you who are new to my books. I continue to learn from you, and to appreciate your steadfast support during my publishing journey.

The Radio Drama

Milford-Haven had its first air date in 1987, and my thanks go to KOTR in Cambria, California, our first radio home. In its next incarnation, *Milford-Haven, U.S.A.* was broadcast on the BBC, for which I thank Ms. Pat Ewing, Director of Radio 5—a maverick network that launched a maverick show and celebrated with us when we reached 4.5 million listeners.

In the U.S., thanks to New York's Museum of TV & Radio and Chicago's Museum of Broadcast Communications, for honoring the show by adding it to their permanent collections. And to Bill Berkuta and Kelly Johnson for helping me create the first Audio Drama Poscast at MilfordHaven.com.

Before there were any shows to air, there were talented actors, and my thanks go to both the original cast of *Milford-Haven* and to the cast of *Milford-Haven, U.S.A.,* seasoned professionals who brought my characters so vividly to life that their work is inextricably woven into the fabric of the characters themselves.

Before there were actors to record, there had to be a studio, and my thanks to Engineer Bill Berkuta, whose Afterhours Recording Company became our studio home—a workshop in which we created one hundred episodes of the first show, sixty of the second, scores of Student Theater & Radio (S.T.A.R.) productions, and now audio books.

Thanks to Marilyn Harris and Mark Wolfram, who composed the haunting *Milford-Haven* theme and all the music cues that supported the emotional ebb and flow of the story, and whose music we now use for the *Milford-Haven Novels* Audio Books.

And before there was a *Milford-Haven,* there was a young woman who had always lived in cities—Tokyo, New York, Los Angeles. I spent a summer performing *Sea Marks* by Gardner McKay at Jim and Olga Buckley's Pewter Plough Playhouse in Cambria, and became fascinated with life in and of a small town.

Thanks to my U.S. listeners, especially those in Cambria and the Central Coast. Thanks to my U.K. listeners, particularly those in Milford Haven, Wales. Both these special towns have embraced me as an honorary citizen.

Thanks to my family and friends—supportive from day one: my late parents Ray & Marshie Purl; Linda Purl, Erin Gray, Caren Pearson, with very special thanks to Miranda Kenrick, and to Vickie Zoellner. My love and thanks to my husband Larry Norfleet.

And finally, thanks to my characters, among whom are: Jack, Zack, Miranda, Zelda, Samantha, Sally, Kevin, Joseph, Cornelius, Meredith, Shelley, June, Chris, Burt, Delmar, Emily, Wilhelm, Stacey, James, Mary, Russell, Nicole, Susan, and Cynthia ... who are building, buying, painting, conniving, planning, dishing, cogitating, dominating, observing, consulting, beach-combing, serving, sleuthing, skulking, detecting, reporting, abusing, enduring, nurturing, scheduling, ordering, showing, sneaking and seducing, respectively.

Dear Reader —

Welcome to Milford-Haven! Whether you're a first-time or a returning visitor, it is my pleasure to introduce you to my favorite little town, but from the unusual perspective of someone who has never lived there, and who has scarcely seen it in daylight.

Journalist Christine Christian follows a lead to Milford-Haven and, against her better judgment (and mine), she drives there in the dead of night to meet a "source" who has promised information valuable enough to topple careers, and maybe dangerous enough to incite murder.

This novella takes Chris—and you—into the unexplored realm of the paranormal, offering what we might call a night-bird's view of the little town that is so filled with hopes and dreams by day, but that roils with nightmares in the dark.

The story stands alone as a complete tale, but is woven into the overall tapestry of the Milford-Haven saga. Chronologically, *What the Soul Suspects* takes place across a span of time that fits against the edges of the novels like the jagged edge of a seismic plate: unstable, unpredictable, but connected at the deepest level, ready to rattle the landscape and spew forth the lava of molten issues.

As this story reveals, Chris is a person who has listened to her head, but ignored her heart—to her own peril. Now she must find a way to share her vital message, and it seems there's only one person capable of listening.

As this novella unfolds, follow my footsteps over the interconnected pathways of those who inhabit, and those who haunt, Milford-Haven, and listen to the guidance that can only be heard when we take seriously . . . what our soul suspects

Mara Purl

"An idea, like a ghost, must be spoken to a little before it will explain itself."

– Charles Dickens

"What terrified me will terrify others; and I need only describe the spectre which had haunted my midnight pillow."

– Mary Shelley

Prologue

The fading sunlight of All Hallows' Eve tiptoed as quietly as a procession of ghosts across Milford-Haven's rugged coastline.

Though hot Santa Ana winds had made the inland hillsides brittle, here along the Central Coast comforting mists rose to cool the headlands. Once-green grasses, now a medley of browns and tans, appeared as smooth as suede stretched across the uneven terrain.

When sun sank into ocean at 5:09, a band of crimson engulfed the edges of the world with deep, barely audible murmurations, leaving the landscape to lost wanderers visible only to themselves.

Their forms glimmered in the 3:02 moonrise on this evening when the veil between the living and the dead was thinnest. As ancient as the Celtic harvest and Gaelic Samhain celebrations, the spirits wandered under a waxing gibbous moon.

A soothsayer would say the Moon in Pisces encouraged perceptiveness of surroundings, where one might experience feelings of insecurity. But not all souls paid attention to warning signs, and they would have to pay the price of altered trajectories.

Tomorrow would be All Souls' Day, the commemoration of all the faithful departed, a day of prayer and remembrance.

But for those who floated through time and space as randomly as driftwood on the tide, there could not yet be remembrance.

There could, however, be awakening.

Chapter 1

Christine Christian couldn't seem to drag herself from the nightmare.

Breathe she kept telling herself. *That's all you have to do. Just breathe.*

With a sharp inhalation, she did just that. *Thank God,* she thought, tamping down the panic that had risen almost too high. She stood in the dark, still shaking, struggling to regain full control. The air seemed close, damp, earthy.

Tiny snicks reached her ears, as though something was falling and hitting the floor . . . or the ground. *What is that? Insects? Lord!* She fought again for control, inhaling slowly, exhaling deliberately. *No, not insects. Dirt. Little pieces of dirt hitting the ground, yes, ground.* She squatted and reached out a hand. Her fingers touched soft, pliant granules and her palm pressed down on spongy earth. When she stood, she felt her face, hair, traced palms down her sleeves, brushing away the remains of . . . what?

A roll in the dirt, apparently. *Did I take a fall? Tumble down a hill? Must have.*

Her next step would have to be a careful one. In the total dark, she couldn't tell whether she now stood at the bottom of whatever hill she'd slid down, or whether she might fall farther. *But where could I be that's this dark? Maybe I'm actually inside something . . . like a cave.*

That thought gave her the creeps—as if she needed more to jangle her nerves. Standing in one place was only leading to more terrifying and useless speculation, so, putting her arms straight in front of her, she began slowly to walk forward. *I feel like Frankenstein's monster. Something to practice for Halloween I guess. Ha ha. When exactly is Halloween? Isn't it still September now? No, no, is it March? Or is it just because I was always afraid of the Ides of?*

Since adding a date-disorientation to her already disordered mind was yet another useless activity, she concentrated on walking. After a few steps she encountered a wall. *This is either great news. Or really bad news.*

At least now she had some physical object to touch other than dirt, a way to reorient her deprived senses. Left hand in contact with the wall, right arm extended in front of her, she continued until the wall ended abruptly, and her ankle made contact with . . . an edge. The edge of a step! So that was it, she'd been in a basement . . . an unfinished one. *The basement of an unfinished house?*

The sudden dizziness nearly made her swoon and she pressed both hands against the wall corner to regain her balance. Images flashed through her brain: soaring walls, sheet-rocked and mudded, but not yet painted; sliding glass doors that threw back dark reflections in the night; high windows angling to an even higher wedge of ceiling.

Is that where I am? Why can't I remember? Must have fallen . . . hit my head. Finally, something made sense. She could feel her breathing calm as the logic took hold. She'd been following a lead. It'd taken her to the unfinished Clarke house. But before she'd been able to meet her mysterious source—the man who'd left a message to meet her here—she'd fallen.

Time to get the hell out of here. As she took the first step, something tightened across her shoulder, yanking her backward. Before thinking, she flung her arm around in a defensive move, but encountered only dead air. "What the—?" One hand braced against the wall, she used the other to feel across her shoulder. "Oh, for God's sake!" she said out loud. "My purse strap!"

In her panic to get out of the claustrophobic space, she'd forgotten about the small purse she wore cross-body when out on assignment. The light canvas zippered bag held only a slender notebook, a couple of pens and pencils, and a folded twenty-dollar bill.

Did I write anything down? Can't remember, and can't see a damn thing. Now the urge to leave clutched at her and she started to race up the stairs, but then realized she might run into a trap door. The last thing she needed was another head injury, so she slowed her pace, raised one hand overhead palm-upward.

As she ascended, faint traces of light reached her dilated pupils, and she arrived at what had to be the main floor. Pin-pricks of pale blue illumination speckled the sub-flooring, where discarded nails and metal shards glinted. Construction debris: one more piece of evidence that made sense, and seemed familiar.

Memory came in disjointed images, like pieces of film picked up from a cutting-room floor. Yes, this was the large room she remembered, with the high angled walls and lots of glass, just as dark now as it had been before. And there was still no sign of her mystery man. *The way I feel right now, I don't even know what I'd ask him. I have to piece things together, maybe retrace my steps.*

A chill came over her. Her intuition had been trying to tell her something when she arrived. To get out! She remembered that now, the internal warning. But she'd failed to heed it and had taken a nasty fall. Maybe even nearly taken a dirt nap. *Well, it was a dirt nap . . . just not a permanent one!*

Tired of the dark, tired of feeling spooked and feeling lost, she craved a beacon of some kind. The moment she stepped out-side, the freshness of cool sea air ruffled her hair, and her nostrils flared at the tang of kelp. *This house is perched right above the ocean.* Waves crashed far below at the back of the property, but where she now stood, a rutted-dirt driveway led away from the front *porte-cochere.*

Turning her head, she saw the familiar flash of the Piedras Blancas lighthouse. That was one good thing about this little town. She'd always liked it. *Milford-Haven. You can see the lighthouse.*

Calm reassurance washed over her like one of the waves she could still hear, the repeating rhythm of the light a steadying beat that seemed to re-synchronize everything that seemed so out of sync.

A beacon of hope . . . a navigational certainty reaching across a troubled sea. I should write that down for a future article. But not now.

Turning away from the flashing light, she realized her next problem would be transportation. *Did I drive here? I must have.* She stepped carefully across the uneven terrain. Then something caught her attention. The black Ford Explorer shone dimly in the starlight, more of an absence than a presence, a black hole the shape of an SUV silhouette. *Thank God.*

She climbed in, worried when the dome light failed to illuminate. The keys were still in the car. *Did I really leave them here?* The vehicle started right up, jerking slightly when she engaged the gears. But the headlights failed to illuminate.

Leaning over, she reached behind the passenger seat and felt for the handle of her work bag. *Yup, there it is. But the car seems to have an electrical short. I'll have to drive carefully . . . maybe head for a sheriff's office, since all the gas stations will be closed so late at night.*

What time it actually was, she couldn't tell, with the dashboard as dark as the rest of the car. Nor did she have a clear idea where to go. A feeling of impatience tugged at her. *Calvin . . . he was waiting.* They were supposed to have dinner . . . probably a make-up from another cancellation. But the last thing she wanted now was dinner. Even less did she relish the idea of the lecture he was bound to spring on her the moment she showed up: "Why would you be out alone so late at night? Why would you go to some deserted house by yourself?" *It's what I do, Calvin,* she would always explain. *I'm an investigative journalist. Sue me.*

Slowly, she nudged the heavy vehicle over the ruts, wound carefully through the unpaved coastal approach road, and finally found herself on Highway 1, pointing north.

Where to go. Truth North. That seems right. And, as if in confirmation, the lighthouse winked in the distance.

In this strangest of nights and oddest of circumstances, logic didn't seem to play as significant a role as intuition in making her decision.

Chapter 2

Delmar Johnson pulled the wrap-around sunglasses off his face and blinked as his eyes adjusted to the relative dimness.

The waiting room of Satellite Station KOST-SATV seemed modest, not nearly as glitzy as he expected. The last television news organization office he'd visited was the NBC building in Burbank, corporate head office for every brand-famous show from *Days of Our Lives* to *The Tonight Show with Jay Leno*.

He glanced around, noting the few details. Chunky oak end-tables, chevron-patterned weave upholstering the heavy couch. He couldn't tell whether the potted plants were real or not. Del sometimes had to remind himself he no longer lived in the big city. *This'd be about right for a regional television office. And besides, satellite is just getting rolling, more of a monkey than the gorilla in the room.*

A young Caucasian woman appeared around the end of the reception desk she'd evidently deserted a few minutes earlier.

"Help you?" she asked.

Del paused for a moment before answering, noting how her gaze traced over his uniform, his badge, and his dark skin.

"Yes. Delmar Johnson, County Sheriff's office. There are some materials ready for me to pick up, some video cassettes? Chris Christian Special Reports?"

She peered down at her desk. "Hmm. I'll have to check on those."

Without another word, she disappeared again. Del glanced down the hallway after her, but saw only a series of closed doors. He strayed to a bulletin board where upcoming event posters made a colorful display.

He heard a door slam, and a moment later the young woman was back, toting a cardboard file box, a slight grimace on her face as she struggled with the weight.

"Here, let me get that." Del took two long steps forward, easily lifting the box from the woman's arms. He made eye contact. "Anything I should sign?"

"Oh! Yes!" She lifted the box top, snatched a piece of paper and replaced the lid.

Del balanced the box on one hip while he used the proffered pen to sign the sheet resting on the counter top. "Thanks. Appreciate it," he said, putting the sunglasses back on, then pushing open the front door.

He placed the box on the passenger-side floor of his departmental SUV, careful to keep the box out of direct sunlight. *These tapes shouldn't stay long in a hot car. Think I'll drop them at the office before I head up to Milford-Haven for dinner.*

Chris Christian drove well below the speed limit—a rarity for her, but with no headlights, she wasn't willing to risk hitting a critter or a pothole in the dark.

Flashes from the lighthouse kept her company when the narrow highway rose a hundred feet above sea-level, but then the comforting beam seemed to wink out when the road dipped, plunging her into consuming darkness.

As she drove, low-lying fog began to creep over the ground, filling first the depressions in the landscape, and finally covering the road itself, until only roadside posts marked the border well enough to keep her on the highway.

Now the Piedras light traced its beacon across the surface of the white-gray fog—tule fog, she suddenly remembered, named after the Chumash word for the reeds once used to build their lodges.

With the fog covering the road, Chris had the peculiar perception that she was driving above the clouds, the landscape beneath now invisible. And all the while, the perfectly timed whirl of the light grew closer, pulling her.

The old lighthouse stood at the end of a long peninsula, shut off from the road by a high fence. It'd been locked the few times she'd tried to visit before, but now she stopped, stepped out of her vehicle and pushed on the gate. To her surprise, it swung inward, and she could dimly see the unpaved road that led to the tower and its adjacent buildings.

Well, what the hell. I might as well take a look, since I've come this far. She drove in, closed the gate behind her, then parked at the base of the concrete structure and craned her neck upward. *It's always been so odd looking for a lighthouse. No beautiful Fresnel adorning its top.* She knew the elaborate first-order light itself, vastly heavy, had been removed for safe-keeping years earlier, leaving the supporting tower looking like a rook in a chess game. The Coast Guard had installed a flasher when they'd automated the light, ending the long custom of live-in lighthouse keepers, but keeping the navigational beam functional.

Chris stepped across the flattened ground surrounding the concrete tower, and gazed straight west, where the flashing light illuminated the off-shore white rocks—the piedras blancas—for which the peninsula was named, noting how they seemed to grow in size for a moment when suddenly bathed in light. Then she faced south and watched as the light flashed over an unfinished house.

That's not just a house, it's the house, the one where I fell. It should be a place of beauty and inspiration, but there's something dark about it . . . literally and figuratively. It's not even finished yet, and already something bad happened there.

The remembrance of waking there in the dark, in the dirt, sent a zing through her as though someone thrummed a bass string attached to her spine. *There was something I was supposed to find, according to that guy who said he'd meet me.*

She struggled to assemble the steps that'd led to that conversation, yet the harder she tried, the more vague the details became, turning to fragments that dissipated like the wisps of surrounding fog. As she watched, the actual fog that'd crept along the highway began to drift toward the distant house, until it shrouded the structure, making it disappear.

Turning away, Chris glanced around. The buildings were dark, save for one soft light that shone through a window. Suddenly worried she wasn't alone, and might be cited for trespassing, she started to walk back to her car. But something made her want to peer through that window. *There it is, that prickly sensation that says there's something for me here.*

She berated herself. *Haven't you had enough trouble for one night? And yet the feeling wouldn't leave her. And didn't I just tell myself that intuition might be more important than logic?*

Before she could think any further, she walked quietly toward the window and cupped her hands as she put her face near the glass. A museum case held various artifacts, no doubt part of the lighthouse history. And a counter stood ready for visitors, brochures neatly stacked.

As she turned to see more clearly, something glinted in the case. Feeling an urge to see what it was, she stepped to the door and quietly turned its handle, surprised when it yielded and the door swung open.

She walked immediately to the case and leaned down. A book—a journal or diary of some kind—with a metal fitting that must have been a lock, rested to one side of it, and the small book lay open, revealing old-fashioned handwriting.

Squinting to see the writing, she saw that on one of the two pages visible, the right side contained only one sentence.

Things are not always what they seem.

The sentence seemed at once simplistic and profound, the kind of thing people said to one another while sharing odd stories. *Well, it sure applies to the night I'm having. Wish I could think of someone to talk to about it.*

But what could it have meant to the author of this journal? Did the lighthouse keeper write it in his log? If so, what would he have been thinking? Or was this a journal kept by his wife?

Breaking into the case to examine the book more closely seemed too intrusive, even for Chris. The sentence, though, seemed worth recording, so she pulled her own notebook from her travel purse, and scribbled it onto the first blank page.

On top of the counter rested several small, loose pieces of scratch paper, bearing various random marks and notes, one of which read, "Point Vicente Next." *Someone jotting down travel plans, I guess. I know there's another lighthouse there.*

Near the notes on the counter she noticed an inking stamp, which she picked up. By the light of the dim bulb, she could see it bore the image of the lighthouse surrounded by a date. *Today's, I imagine, or yesterday's. Visitors use these to stamp their Lighthouse Passports.* Picking it up, she pressed it into the ink pad that lay next to it, then stamped it into her own notebook, not taking the time to read it, but figuring it would be a handy way of noting the date when she assembled her notes, and her thoughts, later.

Time to leave, she exited the building as quietly as she'd entered, closing the door, climbing back into her car, and trundling down the long lane toward the fence.

It didn't seem wise, though, to continue down Highway 1 with no headlights. *I could just sleep in the car till daylight, then head home.*

She imagined that when the black SUV was tucked into the deep shadows of Piedras Blancas, it would seem to disappear into the dark night, not even illuminated by the flashing of the light.

Chapter 3

Delmar had inherited an odd case—sort of. It did involve a crime in the adjacent county to the south, but the crime was against an animal, rather than a human.

To his surprise, a sea otter had been shot to death. The necropsy performed by the Fish & Wildlife man in charge of monitoring the wild population of the southern sea otter along the Central Coast confirmed that the creature had been executed with a pellet gun.

It had been a courtesy to let Del anywhere near the case, but one granted because Del wanted to be sure the forensic information was entered into his own database, in case the weapon used to shoot the otter was later used in a crime against a person, unlikely as that seemed.

His time in Santa Barbara County had been so focused, he hadn't had much time to enjoy the local beauty, nor to touch base with other colleagues. To further limit his activities, the weather had been poor, by Central Coast standards: low 50s with rain, fog, and winds whipping on-shore.

The rain and fog had moved off, though, when Del had stopped for dinner at the Moby Dick Restaurant on the Santa Barbara pier. And there, a strange thing had happened. He'd been sitting at a solo table in the narrow restaurant, gazing out the long row of windows that overlooked the shoreline, when he noticed for the first time how high the surf was. Waves rolled in vigorously, pounding the sand before drawing back for the next hammering.

Suddenly, an even higher and stronger wave struck the row of windows. A woman screamed as a powerful thrust of ocean shattered the glass. The crashing sounds were followed by the slosh of water streaming across the floor.

With apologies, the management hurried to explain they'd have to close, and Del left his half-finished bowl of chowder, along with a twenty-dollar bill, on his table, lifting his feet carefully so as not to slip on his way to the parking lot.

It'd been late when he'd arrived at the restaurant, and he'd been among the last customers for the evening. By the time he left his half-finished meal, he felt too tired to drive all the way to Milford-Haven, so he'd found the motel nearest the marina and bunked in for the night.

He'd slept well enough for the first few hours, but had been awakened by some random sound he couldn't identify. Then he'd tossed and turned, trying to remember the superstitions about breaking glass. *Good luck? Or bad? Well, at least it wasn't a mirror that broke.*

Breakfast had been a much more successful meal, enjoyed at Max's, the wonderful little locally-owned café he'd found a few months earlier. When he left there, he was near the entrance to the Pass, so he'd decided to take that route home to save a little time.

The San Marcos Pass—highway 154—was a favorite for its spectacular views. But the road could be treacherous, a narrow serpentine that wound through the mountain range rising suddenly above Santa Barbara, and formed a gateway to the Santa Inez Valley. Accidents along parts of this road were legendary, and he always kept a sharp lookout, particularly driving an official sheriff-department vehicle.

But today the 154 was resplendent with blooming wild-flowers racing down the hillsides, and the Pacific sparkling far below. Once he crested over the mountain and arrived in the wide valley beyond, he glanced right and left as his SUV sped by some of California's most gorgeous horse ranches. The region was famous for pristine breeding barns, and people claimed that at least one horse-whisperer practiced in one of these ranches.

A city-boy who hailed from the mean streets of South Central Los Angeles, Del's equine knowledge could fit into a thimble—or whatever its equivalent would be in the horse world. Horses did possess a mystique, but he found the idea of being too close to a thousand-pound animal a challenge he didn't care to take on.

Fortunately, Del hadn't found himself stuck behind a slow hay-truck during this run on the narrow road, where passing opportunities were few. The smaller mountain road deposited him onto the 101, and he pressed his accelerator till he reached the higher speed limit. His boss had called a meeting of the SPU at eleven this morning. The Special Projects Unit to which he'd been assigned was a perfect career match for Del, giving him the chance to tackle some unusual assignments and, for the most part, managing his own schedule, rather than punching a time clock.

Still, being late to a Unit meeting was not an option. *Good thing I'm making good time.*

Chris Christian woke curiously refreshed after her strange night. She knew there was a gas station not far from Piedras, where she could use the facilities and fill the car with fuel. Granted, the station was north—the wrong direction—but she felt too disheveled to stop at an eatery in San Simeon or Milford-Haven, so she chose to go slightly out of her way.

She found the site deserted, the gas station long-since closed. Fortunately, she didn't need fuel after all, and the restroom was still there, so she availed herself, but found no mirror to check her face and hair. She left the eerie place quickly, traveling Highway 1 south till it met the 101, then picking up speed as she continued south.

It suddenly seemed like a long time since she'd been home. This wasn't so unusual. She often spent weeks away on assignment, living out of a suitcase and making cheap motel rooms into makeshift offices with her portable computer. Her unpredictable travel schedule was the reason she used to pay her rent months in advance, then had eventually purchased the condo and paid her maintenance fee a year forward as a lump sum.

She found herself looking forward to the comforts available at her Santa Maria condo. Modest by some standards— certainly by those of her sometime boyfriend Calvin. *Why do I always call him by his last name? Anyway, the man has a mansion, an estate overlooking the Pacific in Santa Barbara. But... it's oil money. Never been sure how I feel about that.*

And she couldn't imagine how he felt about her digs, so meager by comparison. Still, for her own purposes, the California stucco offered a small office where she kept her files, a portable computer with a docking station, and an archive of work notebooks. Her modest kitchen, dining, and "great room" were comfortable with neutral colors and a gas fireplace. And her small bedroom held an enormous bed with first-class linens. *Ahhh... that's what's gonna feel fine tonight.*

While thinking about getting home, she found she'd made good time on the road, where there wasn't much traffic. She glanced left and noticed in the distance an approaching SUV even larger than her own. *An official car. Sheriff's department? If this were last night, he'd be doing a U-turn to give me a citation.*

As the cop car drew closer, she found her gaze turning repeatedly toward the driver—a man, she could see, with dark skin. And then they made eye contact, and their vehicles seemed to pass one another in slow motion.

That face ... so handsome! Do I know him? I feel like I do. I don't remember meeting him. But I've seen him.

Normal time resumed, and Chris brought her attention back to the road, not knowing what to make of the connection. *Well . . . if I see him again, I'll recognize him.*

Chapter 4

Delmar gripped the wheel of the Durango so hard, his knuckles turned pale. *What white folks call white-knuckling.*

His mind raced, trying to process the face he'd just seen through that oncoming windshield. *Blond, chiseled, elegant.* The face was familiar. But he was sure she wasn't someone he'd met. So his memory shifted to the series of current sketches the department was circulating: suspects for whom APBs had been issued; recent victims; missing persons.

Though he prided himself on his skill at tracking and comparing cross-platform visual recognition from sketch to flesh, and from photographs of the living to the dead, he couldn't summon an I.D. of the woman he'd just seen.

What, then? What had tripped his imagination, caught his attention?

Then an odd thought struck him. His mother had sometimes spoken about meeting his father. "They say love at first sight don't exist. But it does. It happened to your father and me."

Del had taken it with a grain of salt, assuming it was more romanticized memory than reality. But perhaps his mother really had experienced the phenomenon.

Might it be possible the person he'd just seen was her—the woman of his dreams, the one he was supposed to meet? Could there really be such a thing as love at first sight?

If so, the moment had literally flashed by him so quickly, it was gone almost the instant it arrived.

Chris felt more relieved to be at home than she could have imagined. After a cursory glance through the rooms to ensure everything was in order, she headed for her bedroom, where she was surprised to find the bed unmade.

Oh yeah . . . I think I left in a hurry. The sheets, cool and soft to the touch, seemed so inviting. *After sleeping in my car, I deserve a nap.* She kicked off her shoes, pulled her legs out of her slacks, and slipped into the high-threadcount cotton.

Chris slid into the dream seamlessly, and believed that when she woke into the December interlude, it was happening in real time.

Chris threw back the covers after a short nap, and stepped to the closet, where her party dress hung ready for tonight's festivities.

She took extra care with her make-up and hair, eager to make a good impression on Calvin and his ritzy friends. This was also supposed to be the first time she'd stay at his Calma estate longer than one night, and she'd packed a couple of outfits and even thrown in a holiday sweater.

When she pulled the party dress on, it turned her into a shimmering column of silver topped with an upsweep of golden hair. The gold-and-silver twisted cable jewelry wound together the two metallics perfectly.

She slipped her arms into her long, white wool coat, lifted her overnight bag, and headed for her garage. Two hours later, she was stepping out of the car, assisted by an attendant in the Calma driveway.

The home, festooned with seasonal decor, already held more guests than Chris imagined would be there. They strode through the foyer then migrated down a long corridor she remembered led to the rear of the house, the patio and the garden. Chris watched as guests greeted one another with small pleasantries, and sampled canapes as wait staff circulated. She longed for a glass of champagne, but didn't want to imbibe until she'd found her host. She wanted to see in his eyes his appreciation of her dress, hear his voice whisper something provocative, feel him pull her close.

She stepped for a moment into Calvin's office, surprised to see a man sitting opposite the large desk. Actually, the dark figure didn't seem to be a party guest. He sat poised with a notebook as if ready to ask questions.

Curious, she wished the man would turn around so she could see his face, and suddenly he did turn. But, embarrassed at the idea of being caught watching him, she stepped quickly to one side of the open doorway.

None of my business, she told herself. Now I really must find Calvin . . . but I better remember to call him Joseph.

Live music sounded from the rear of the house, and she followed the sound till she saw the tented back yard, sparkling with tiny white lights. This party just goes on and on.

And then she glimpsed him at last, surrounded by guests, smiling. She tried to catch his eye just by standing still, but realized her pale gown would be lost in the medley of bright holiday colors worn by the other women.

So she walked closer, smiling at him, until she saw the woman standing next to him. Who is that? Raven-haired, voluptuous, draped—no, shrink-wrapped—in blue that shimmers purple in the lights. And she certainly has his full attention.

Chris's first instinct was to swoop between them, kiss Calvin full on the mouth, and stake her claim. She realized, though, that she had no idea who this woman was, nor how important she might be to him. A business contact? A partner's wife?

Joseph seemed caught off guard, as though he were trying to get a handle on some sort of undercurrent. Then, as though he suddenly remembered his manners, he said, "Cynthia, have you met Zelda McIntyre?"

Chris wasn't quite close enough to hear the two women, facing away from her now, exchanging what must have been polite comments. But once again, Joseph couldn't seem to think of what to say next. Time seemed to slow as the awkward absence of commentary isolated the small group in the midst of a sea of conversations. Like they're caught in the eye of a storm.

The lull in the conversation between Calvin, the woman, and that younger couple gave Chris an opening. "Joseph," she said, "It's good to see you."

For a moment, he glanced in her direction, but he just stood there, frozen.

"My long drive went fine, thanks for asking," she wanted to say. "And thanks for noticing my dress. Where did you want me to put my overnight bag?"

Everyone in the small circle looked down for a moment, as though trying to cover their embarrassment. And then Joseph Calvin focused again on his purple-clad guest, ignoring Chris completely.

For the next minute, Chris was too shocked to react. "Seriously?" she wanted to shout. "This is how you want to treat me? I mean, I know I've been the absentee girlfriend for a while, but I thought we had an understanding."

Clearly, Calvin understood nothing at all. Turning on her heel, Chris strode back into the house with as much control as she could muster. She walked by the office again, glimpsing the waiting stranger who now stood by a wall of bookshelves.

Chris, starved for the connection she'd come here to make, longed to say something to the stranger. She felt some resonance, perhaps because both of them were being ignored. He was too handsome not to be circulating among the beautiful people at the party, but he wasn't dressed for the occasion and seemed too focused to waste his time with small talk. He's here on some sort of mission. Business? Legal? Maybe even law enforcement?

Her reporter-skills kicked in, and she made mental notes of his physical features: dark-skinned, broad-shouldered, long-legged, well-muscled: all of that apparent even though she could only see him in profile. Then, long fingers reached for a small frame on one of the book shelves. When he turned it in his hand, she saw it was a photo of herself with the master of the manse.

Instantly, her mental coolness fled and hot temper flooded her system. Chris wanted to snatch the photo, hurl it across the room. But just then the stranger touched the image of her face. The wistful gesture made her heart ache. "If you turned around, you'd see me in the flesh," *she whispered, choking on the words.*

She wanted to shout, "Go arrest him for rudeness and stupidity, will you? Tell him he's an idiot not to recognize a good thing when he has it in the palm of his hand. Tell him it's . . . it's slipping away."

But if she spoke to this man, what would she really say? She would only subject herself to questions. Instead, Chris turned from the humiliating scene and continued to the foyer, where she retrieved her coat from the long, portable rack sagging with furs and elegant woolens. Then she continued to the front steps, handed her claim ticket to a valet, climbed into her car, and began the long drive home.

Chapter 5

Delmar had let go of that quick flash of almost-recognition that'd happened on the highway earlier, and focused on the details of his Unit meeting.

His boss, Captain Sandoval, customarily had interesting updates to share with his crew, and always treated Del not only as a true equal—just the way he treated all the members of his Special team—but also as someone with specialized insights about gangs, having dealt with them for several years in South Central.

Though a man of action, Del was also a man of words, and it often struck him that word "central" was like a recurring theme for him: he'd moved from South Central L.A. to the Central Coast. *And the two locations have nothing at all in common, except that word, he mused. Except ongoing danger from gangs.*

Psychologists and sociologists pointed to a host of related issues as root causes: absence of strong father-figures in the lives of young boys; poverty, deprivation, and lack of legacy savings and ownership; hatred and fear; poor language skills. And at the base of it all, Del always felt a toxic slurry of racism poisoned the water drunk by everyone on both sides, the haves and the have-nots.

What allowed gang activities and membership to expand and even flourish was the sense of belonging and financial success that came with membership—short-lived as these almost always were. Respect, a sense of power, and the pride of having some "cake" to spend puffed up a boy enough that he could feel like a man for a little while.

Here in the Central Coast, where the racial mix was primarily Caucasian and Hispanic, Del stuck out like an oddity, but at least his boss, and most of his unit-colleagues treated him with respect, though only one had so far invited him out for a beer.

Today's update had included a run-down of local crimes— zero murders, and among the lowest numbers for rape or aggravated assault by L.A. standards. The Unit tended to inherit cold cases, those involving long, involved white-collar scams sometimes requiring forensic accounting expertise; and missing persons which, so far, seemed to land on Del's desk.

He'd closed one such case a few weeks earlier. An elderly man who'd recently moved to Paso Robles, had gotten in his car one morning and simply driven away. His wife had feared that dementia had caused him to forget their new address, and that he might be trying to return to their former home.

It turned out the wife was partially correct: the man had returned home. But evidently it wasn't because of failing memory. He'd returned to their former town to reconnect with the long-time mistress about whom the wife had never known.

"Never too old,"Del's colleagues had joked when he shared the details. But the case had rather a grim ending. The wife showed up at the trailer park where her husband and his girlfriend had settled, and shot them both. Now two senior citizens were dead, and the third would spend her few remaining years in lock-up, one way or another.

Del had an open missing-person case now, one that he'd had to set aside for a while, what with more urgent business pushing it farther and farther down his work pile. No corpse had shown up, and nothing about the missing woman's life really seemed particularly out of order. She often traveled on long assignments, and there were no solid, legal grounds for digging into her personal life when she might, in fact, turn up any day.

Still, Del felt by turns intrigued and concerned, enough so that he'd requested to review some of her professional work. He felt a bit guilty at the prospect of viewing the videos that now waited at his office. But, she was a broadcast journalist, and he had only asked to watch work that had already been shown publicly, so he wasn't breaking any privacy laws.

As Del drove home to Milford-Haven for a quick dinner, he flashed back to an interview he'd conducted with Joseph Calvin last December. Calvin had apparently once dated the woman, and had called the Department, saying he felt some concern at her absence.

The informal conversation held at Calvin's home office had gone well enough. Afterward, the two men had gone so far as to walk through the woman's apartment in Santa Maria, to which Calvin had a key. They'd found nothing amiss, except perhaps the presence of a set of packed suitcases.

But frequent travelers often kept some bags pre-packed so they'd be ready to depart at a moment's notice, so the suitcases proved nothing.

Del had made one more appearance at the Calvin estate, trying for an unannounced visit, so as not to give the man any chance to prepare for a second conversation.

The evening Del had chosen, however, hadn't worked well, because Mr. Calvin had been entertaining that night. And it hadn't just been an intimate dinner party. It'd been a "blow-out" as the press later called it, a charity shindig with an A-list of guests from the Santa Barbara social register. Del thought back to that evening, reviewing the sequence of events, almost surprised to remember it in such detail.

Del had been shown into Calvin's office, on the night in question, by a butler who, though efficient, clearly seemed more than fully occupied with keeping the evening on track.

After sitting alone in the home office for a few minutes, Del wandered as unobtrusively as possible through the house and grounds. He recognized a couple of people. One was Miranda Jones, the artist from Milford-Haven. Another was a woman named Zelda McIntyre whose photo he'd seen in local papers.

He caught a glimpse of another woman. For a moment, he thought she might been the prodigal journalist returned. Trim and blond, sheathed in some sort of iridescent dress, the woman slipped through the crowd like a person on a mission. *Like a silver bullet speeding toward a target.* Del thought he'd try to get to her to introduce herself and find out who she was, but she'd been too quick for him.

Back in Calvin's office, he tried for patience as he began another bout of waiting. Sensing a presence just behind him, he glanced over his shoulder. *No one's there now...but someone was there a moment ago.* Rationalizing, he decided that with party guests arriving every few seconds, one of them must've peeked into this room.

Though Del had been here quite recently for his meeting with the mansion's owner, Joseph Calvin was obviously fully engaged this evening. Del wasn't sure the man would leave his guests even for a few minutes.

So he availed himself of the chance to look around Mr. Calvin's home office. Though he'd conducted his previous interview in this very room, his primary focus had been Calvin's facial expressions and body language—not his possessions. Now he looked more closely at the knick-knacks and bound volumes filling the mahogany shelves, the sleek silver letter opener that appeared as sharp as a dagger, the array of Cross pens marching along in a felt-lined case.

What interested Del most were the plethora of photographs. Beautifully framed—some in silver, some in leather-clad wood— they stood on shelves, credenza, and occasional tables situated next to the upholstered chairs that offered conversational seating.

Calvin's son, Zachary, was featured in many of the shots: as a boy of twelve, holding a soccer ball; as a gangly teen holding a tennis racket; as a young stud aboard a sail boat. Then there were father-and-son shots at various points in the boy's life, including one of the proud father with his newly minted Harvard grad, and another of the two grown men wearing hardhats on what appeared to be an off-shore oil rig. *Talk about privilege. Are they even aware of how much they have? What charmed lives they lead?*

Apart from the set of family photos, Del discovered a bound album with clippings from the Society pages: Joseph at assorted charity functions, a stylish woman on his arm in each—several of them blond—but never the same woman. *Must be nice. But I wonder if it gets old after a while.*

Delmar had been wandering through every corner of Calvin's office for several minutes when he came across a frame that'd been laid flat, and partially concealed on a shelf behind the back of a tall chair. He picked it up and saw the image of Joseph Calvin with yet another blonde. At first, he assumed this was just another of his society dates. But then, perhaps this was the long-lost Chris Christian? Hard to tell, as she wore a hat. Whoever she was, these were happy times, evidently, as both of them beamed aboard a sailboat on a bright, sunny day.

He wanted to stare at the image, take it closer to a better light source, but something else drew his attention. Catching a glimpse of something shimmering just at the edge of the open doorway, he decided to stand still and wait. His muscles quivered with the effort and he slowed his breathing. *Maybe this is the same person who stood here a few minutes ago. Maybe this time she'll say something.*

But he—or she—hadn't, if the person had ever been there at all.

Del brought his attention back to the road, wondering what had set his mind to reviewing that party from last December.

Oh! It's because the woman on the highway coming the other direction reminded me of the one I saw at Calvin's party. Okay, that makes sense.

Del hadn't realized a part of his brain had still been working to identify that face that flashed by as their vehicles passed one another. "You gotta find somethin' that'll take your mind off work sometimes, Hon," his mother Ruby used to say.

"You're right, Mom. One of these days, I'll get a life."

Del's keys jangled as he unlocked the door to his rented house, and he inhaled the mixture of pine, eucalyptus and sea air, an elixir to which he'd quickly become addicted for its therapeutic properties.

Sighing as he pushed through the door and locked it behind him, he yanked off his sturdy work shoes, removed his weapon, holster, and belt to hang them in the locked closet near this door, the back way that led from his garage to the small home's interior.

Following his usual ritual, he showered, changed into sweats, pulled on heavy socks and sat down at his kitchen table to review the files he'd brought home. Among the papers, he came across Chris Christian's journal. He'd been delaying the review of the private writings, but now the time felt right at least to peruse the pages.

The notebook was small, and came with an elastic strap, so it'd be something she carried with her, maybe in a pocket or purse. And it was full, labeled on its front page as 1996-C. That suggested there might be an A or a B notebook somewhere, but those hadn't been recovered at her home.

He opened the small cover and noticed an aroma rising from the flyleaf. *Something herbal? Something she usually wears, probably.* He turned the first page, guilty about intruding into the thoughts she'd have recorded here, ideas she had not intended anyone else to see. Her handwriting began in a clear hybrid of printing and cursive, but gradually devolved into a kind of personal shorthand, as though the thoughts were coming so fast she couldn't keep up.

Now he could see these were a kind of index for her adoption story, numbers and letters that apparently referred to interview questions and observations. These would make an interesting counterpoint to the video footage he'd be watching, especially if he could find the actual notes to which they referred. Even if they didn't reveal any data not included in her broadcast, the notes might reveal something of her process.

He flipped forward to the middle of the book, confirming she was still on the same topic. *Did she use a dedicated notebook for each topic? Or was her note-taking more opportunistic, such that she jotted down any and everything that came to mind?*

Still not quite willing to read the book from cover to cover, he rifled through the pages. The entries seemed to be a combination of scrawled text, rough drawings, pasted-in labels, and images from rubber stamps. What this eclectic collection could possibly mean, he couldn't immediately grasp but two sensations hit him at once. He huffed out a small laugh at the inherent whimsy this woman captured on the fly during the course of a busy, professional life. And he nearly choked at the possibility that her originality might have been snuffed out.

But we don't know that, he reminded himself.

Now something else struck him: the little book had a density to it, as though it contained so much information it would take time and concentration to unpack. A quick perusal wouldn't suffice. But before he set it aside, he had to find out what the rubber stamp image might be.

He found the relevant page easily and peered at it. A faded line-drawing, with some missing edges showed a lighthouse inside a circular frame. He looked more closely and saw that slightly smudged words read "Piedras Blancas Light Station."

That made sense. Like many people in the area, she evidently enjoyed visiting lighthouses. No big mystery there. He held the book directly under the light, and saw the faint image of a round date stamp next to the lighthouse image. The date was October 31,

1996—Halloween of the previous year. Now he reached for his own notepad and jotted down the date and location. He could check the dates of her broadcasts, perhaps request more from her television studio, and also plug in appointments from her own calendar . . . if and when this became an official investigation. For now, he'd add what he could to his own Chris file.

It seemed she was rather informal in her pursuit of following lighthouses, because this stamp wasn't in an official Lighthouse Passport, it was stuck in amongst various other journal entries. Still, it meant enough to her to retain as a keepsake.

Was this sentimental? Or was Chris Christian beginning to do research on lighthouses for some future program? He'd have to discover the answer to that question another time. For tonight, the rest of his stack of files beckoned, and he knew he was too tired to stay up much longer.

Chapter 6

Chris woke with a start, disoriented, heart racing. She began to calm when she saw she was in her own bed, but confused when she didn't see her overnight bag, nor the silver gown hung on the edge of the closet door.

Sitting up, she saw the last of golden light seeping through her blinds, coming from the west. *So . . . it's not the morning after that holiday party. Was that was just a dream? Yes, but a memory dream with all the details.* She looked around. *Anyway, now it's late afternoon or early evening, and I'm waking up from a nap.*

Shaking her head and blinking a few times, she decided a hot shower might be the cure for the ongoing confusion she felt. As she stepped into the soothing stream of water and ran fingers through her hair, she winced when they traced over a knot on the back of her head. *No wonder! I really did take a wallop when I fell.*

Rather than continue to worry, she decided to give herself a break. After all, it wasn't every day a person fell into a hole and spent a night sleeping in dirt. She no longer felt dizzy, there was no open wound, and she was beginning to feel better. The hard knock she must've given her head seemed to explain her symptoms.

Refreshed after her shower, Chris pulled on a comfy set of gray sweats and let her towel-dried hair drip a bit onto the collarless top. She pushed up her sleeves, dotted her wrists with the lavender oil she always found soothing, and she went to the kitchen to make coffee—one thing she always kept on hand—then took a steaming mug to her office.

Sitting in her desk chair, she swivelled for a moment, her gaze moving over her work surface—one place that was always neat, except when she was in the throes of writing a story.

Most of her colleagues had substantial desktop computers in their home offices, but because of her mobile lifestyle, Chris had opted for a Sony VAIO notebook computer. When she was home, she snapped it into its docking station, which included a CD/DVD player and multiple printer ports. Even then, it was only two-and-a-quarter inches thick and light enough to haul around her condo. Sony had introduced the line this year and it stood for Visual Audio Integrated Operation. The term was a little too technical for her, but the machine wasn't.

When she traveled, at least on shorter jaunts, she just carried the "notebook" itself: one-and-a-quarter inch thickness, inputs for mini-disk, headphones, microphone, and pretty much anything else she might need.

She looked at it now—sleek, silver, compact—and flashed back to her original "laptop": a Hermes Rocket portable typewriter. She'd taken it everywhere during her early reporter days, most notably on the Apollo Soyuz assignment, during which she'd festooned the removable cover with NASA stickers that advertised the mission. Unlike most typewriters, it had a flat bottom that literally allowed her to type while balancing it on her lap. That'd proved handy when she'd been interviewing VIPs on bleachers in the hot Florida sun prior to the Kennedy Space Center launch.

I've come a long way, she thought. The VAIO was as much a leap forward as was the Shuttle from the Soyuz. The technology made her so much more efficient, she could no longer imagine life without it.

Her gaze continued across her desk area. Research files were kept in their drawers; active files were kept in labeled folder held by black metal desktop racks. One entire rack was filled with her "Seismic" folders, each of which held a sub-category: Los Angeles; Japan; Turkey; Central Coast; Chile; Hawaii. Her research was well under way, but she still had quite a bit of travel and follow-up to complete.

She'd had a great meeting with the lead seismologist at Cal Tech in Pasadena a few weeks earlier. To prepare for that meeting, Chris had studied seismology texts and articles in the library, really living with the subject to understand better the difference between slip and thrust strikes, the overall picture of the movement of the Pacific Plate and the relative stability of the North American Plate—the two giant land masses that met along the San Andreas fault line.

She'd read *Assembling California* by the great author John McFee, published just three years earlier in 1993, and come to understand so much better the plate-dynamics of her home state.

Suddenly it occurred to her that her story did not yet include any sort of correlation between earthquakes and lighthouses, and that mapping lighthouse damage could be an interesting snapshot of seismic activity in California, and perhaps elsewhere.

She recalled that the Piedras Blancas light had suffered through a 4.6 temblor on New Year's Eve 1948, necessitating not only the removal of its first-order Fresnel, but also its top three stories, leaving it as it now appeared, a rook rather than a queen on the coastal chess board.

Those details would certainly enhance her report. "Point Vicente Next." That note she'd found in the museum case at Piedras popped back into her mind. Still unsure what that'd meant to the person who'd scribbled it, she began to feel it actually made sense as a directive for her to follow.

She never embarked on a research trip, however, without first doing her homework. *This is why I keep an archive of files in my home office,* she thought, though various bosses and colleagues had always scoffed, telling her everything she'd ever need could be found at a good library.

The racks atop her desk holding the active seismic folders didn't include anything about Point Vicente, so she pulled out the file drawer and began searching through the S's. "Seismic" held twenty or thirty sub-categories. *Pretty sure I have one with lists of California coastal quakes.* "Ha!" she said aloud with smug satisfaction. "Got it."

Sure enough, a few years ago she'd asked her contact at Cal Tech for a print-out of "events" along the coast, and she skimmed through the listings, which were organized by city, with distances to epicenters in kilometers.

She looked down the list for Palos Verdes—the location of the Point Vicente light.

2.6 in March 1986 2 km W of Rancho Palos Verdes

3.5 in October 1970 1 km W of Rancho Palos Verdes

2.8 in April 1944 6 km E of Rancho Palos Verdes

4.7 in October 1940 8 km WSW of Palos Verdes Estates

Anything "West" of Palos Verdes would be offshore and under water. The only earthquake sizable enough to have caused damaged at the nearest lighthouse would have happened in 1940.

Now Chris cross-referenced with her series of "Lighthouse" files. Sure enough, the lighthouse in question was located in the Palos Verdes Fault Zone—and the underwater maps showed a fractured sea floor to prove the point. Details in the report gave a pretty clear outline.

Type of Faulting: right-reverse

Length: roughly 80 km

Nearby Communities: San Pedro, Palos Verdes Estates,
        Torrance, Redondo Beach

Most Recent Surface Rupture: Holocene, offshore; Late
        Quaternary, onshore

Slip Rate: between 0.1 and 3.0 mm/yr

Interval Between Major Ruptures: unknown

Probable Mangitudes: MW6.0 - 7.0 (or greater?); fault geometries may
allow only partial rupture at any one time
Other Notes: Has two main branches. Continues southward as the Palos
Verdes-Coronado Bank fault zone.

If she visited this lighthouse, would she find someone knowledgeable to interview? Probably. Would she learn anything new? Perhaps not. Still, seeing it in person could only enhance her understanding. *And who knows? Maybe my next piece will be about lighthouses. I seem to be developing a thing for them.*

Chapter 7

Del flipped on the lights in the conference room and placed his cardboard storage box on the big table.

He'd put in a long day, but it'd all been inside, for a change, and that'd given him a chance to do some serious catch-up on paper work.

With no particular plans for the evening, he'd decided tonight would be a good time to review the videotapes he'd picked up from KOST. He walked toward the rolling stand that held the television and videocassette player, then leaned down to fire up the VCR.

He shook his head remembering that he—the unit's tech nerd—had struggled at first to learn this technology. Well, in fairness, he was proficient at computers but had no home videotape machine, so wasn't accustomed to scheduling the recording of favorite programs. He had no time for such amusements. But now, realizing how much research could actually be done by pre-taping specific broadcast offerings, or by borrowing tapes from the library or elsewhere, he'd begun to consider buying a set-up for himself.

Del hit the Play button on the VCR, then turned off the over-head recessed canister lights, which plunged the room into an eerie blue glow cast by the television monitor. Then white letters appeared on the screen, giving the title and details of the program —obviously in-house designations, rather than opening credits that'd be shown on-air.

And then, suddenly, there she was: Christine Christian in the flesh . . . or, in the transmission waves—the radiating electrical signal—he amended. Through the available technology, she became a vivid presence that had him shuddering with some unidentifiable resonance.

It was when she walked toward the camera and he got a better look at her that a jolt of electricity traveled down his own spine. Yes, this would be the woman whose photograph he'd seen at Joseph Calvin's office. But this also might be the woman whose face had flashed past him as their cars traveled in opposite directions on the 101.

With such a brief glimpse, he couldn't be sure. *Still . . . what the hell?* If she was driving around the Central Coast, she certainly wasn't missing. *Was she in hiding? Or am I now so obsessed with this cold case that my mind is playing tricks on me?*

Del hit the Pause button and tried to calm himself. Ghostly light reflected onto the slatted blinds. The image of the reporter —crisp, animated, and *alive*—disturbed him. To give himself a few seconds' break he glanced at the pale gray walls offset by black trim and looked up at the unilluminated bulbs that stared back like glassy, unseeing eyes. He turned back to the TV, hit Play and watched the screen as the camera zoomed in on Chris's face.

The more he watched the videos—with as detached a perspective as he could—the more he realized the journalist had that classic almost cookie-cutter style that on-air personalities seemed to cultivate: flawless, regular features, clean jaw lines, sculpted nose, and eyes that could bore a hole through the screen. Her air-brushed make-up, smooth blunt-cut hair, even her well-modulated voice all seemed calculated to have her seem professional enough to trust, but never more interesting than the story she was covering. *She's designed to disappear.* And that was an eerie thought.

"Will This Love Last?" was the title of Segment I, in which Chris—he suddenly thought of her as "Chris" now, rather than "Subject Christian" or some more formal appellation—began to delve deeply into an issue to which he'd never given much thought. *But she's drawing me in.* That's her skill, he began to realize—to catch the attention of her audience, create connections that played across the viewers' heartstrings, then reel them in.

Yet the purpose of *his* viewing the tapes was not to learn about the subjects she reported, but to glean information about the reporter herself. If she presented a calm facade, did anything seem to rattle her? Did her style reflect more raw ambition, pushing forward her own career agenda? Or did it reveal a genuine interest in her subjects and in bringing them to her followers?

"Adoption," said Chris in her news-voice. "It's one of the most consuming interests among Americans today." She stepped toward a swing and sat carefully in its leather strap. "Approximately three thousand five hundred children are adopted annually in the United States, with the trend rising more than 80 percent since 1990, the year November was named National Adoption Month. And the rules have changed.

"Adoption used to be a private and irrevocable matter. If you, as a parent, gave up your child for adoption, you knew you would never see that child again. You also knew it would be better for the child not to suffer the confusion of meeting a parent he or she had never known.

"Tonight we take you on the first of a three-part journey into the mysteries and emotional turmoil of adoption. If you adopt a child, will he or she truly be yours forever?"

After a brief pause, a flash of white letters reading INSERT COMMERCIAL A filled the screen, and Del immediately pressed the Pause button. Already, he could tell the program would be good, and that he'd be drawn even further into the subject the journalist had chosen.

He also knew he was already fighting to keep objectivity, and he couldn't yet put his finger on why. Something about this woman engaged him. The fascination with cases was one of his own qualities that he knew well, and he recognized the symptoms of that particular contagion. But something was at work even deeper in his psyche.

Suddenly exhausted, he needed his bed, needed to escape this room that'd become a chamber of illusive clues and fleeting familiarity, a gaseous mixture of wild guesses and cold hard facts.

It was as though the room existed between realities. He had to return to his own as quickly as possible.

Chapter 8

Chris had no idea why the headlights in her SUV had somewhat magically started working again. She'd come out to her carport to check, unwilling to drive in the dark again if they weren't functioning. In that case, she'd have begun her trek at first light tomorrow, but now she decided missing the heavy traffic through Santa Maria, then Santa Barbara, then L.A. itself would give her an advantage.

The comfortable Explorer was like a second home—her "Ford Living Room," as she liked to call it. To keep away various smells that could accumulate in its interior, she kept a small sachet of lavender in the otherwise unused ashtray. She reached for the radio dial, but found that, unlike the headlights, the radio wasn't working and she got nothing but static. She snapped it off and considered using her right hand to reach behind the front seat to rummage in her CD carrier for something to listen to. After a moment or two, that seemed like too much trouble, and she re-centered herself in the driver's seat.

She glanced eastward to the mountains, noting how the last of the light tinted the ridges a dark blood-red while leaving a deep

Prussian blue canopy overhead. On the road, a steady stream of headlights headed north but southbound traffic was light.

Sure of her route for the moment, and with nothing to do but follow the highway, she let her mind begin to wander back to this afternoon's vivid dream.

That woman in the dream, the one Joseph seemed to be with. Voluptuous, intense. Such an opposite type from me. But he seemed so taken with her, even to the point of absolutely ignoring me.

The more Chris thought about that awkward situation, the more irritated she became, all the more so because she couldn't determine whether it was a memory, or a dream. If it was a dream, maybe it included a couple of interesting clues. First, it seemed likely that Joseph saw other women, even while seeing her, and the more absent she was, the more likely. Second, the woman at the party apparently made her jealous. *Really? Does that mean I care more about Joseph than I thought?*

When the sign appeared for mountain highway 154, she decided to take it, edging into the right lane for the left-looping overpass. After several miles, she began carefully nosing the car through the winding turns of the San Marcos Pass, and inhaling when the view opened up to the sparkling lights of Santa Barbara far below.

When her thoughts came back to Joseph, she realized her irritation was not over his attentions to another woman, but rather over the fact that he hadn't been honest with her. Was Joseph the love of her life? No. Neither did she imagine he had strong feelings for her, either. Instead, their pleasant series of connections had represented some sort of potential—one they were never likely to fulfill.

Maybe it truly was a dream, she decided, and that's what the dream was really about—giving herself permission to let go, and to let him find someone who lived nearby, ran in his social circles, and would be willing to commit.

Ah, the "c" word . . . one she'd managed to avoid her whole life, at least on the personal level. Maybe, once upon a time and long, long ago, there'd been a thundering love that'd stampeded through her heart and carried her away. But no one could handle a multi-racial relationship back then—not her family, not his, not their school nor their neighborhoods.

They were so young when it started, it'd been dismissed as "puppy love" by their elders. They could've been trailblazers, she and Ron—taken their private vision and their secret love into the big, bad world. But they'd have had to do so without the support of family, friends, or society at large. If they'd been born even a decade later, the tide would already have begun to change and they might have been carried on the new wave. As it was, they'd each believed the wisdom hammered into them, allowing their families and mentors to heave sighs of relief and do their best to put distance between their homegrown Romeo and Juliet.

Why would I think of him now? I haven't thought of him in years. Well . . . not consciously anyway, though she knew he often visited her dreams, and likely always would. Chris shook her head as if the gesture could chase away the empty reverie.

She pulled to a stoplight in Santa Barbara, where the highway blended into a local street. To her right, the harbor lights twinkled and the pier invited tourists to late suppers, but when the traffic signal turned green, she accelerated and soon the sumptuous homes of the rich and beautiful slipped past.

By now she'd traveled more than half the distance to her destination and her mind began focusing on this series that was dimly beginning to take shape in her thought. Lighthouses: California icons, treasure-troves of local history ripe for study and discovery.

There were "lighthouse people" she knew, devotees who arranged elaborate and extensive travel to visit as many as they could. And she now knew one could acquire a Lighthouse Passport, a little collector's booklet to create as a personal keepsake.

But her own television audience was far broader than these focused obsessives, so she'd have to make the case for the masses, showing them that California offered specialized museums, each with spectacular views and probably devastating stories of loss and perhaps salvation.

She'd read about the Point Vicente light she was about to visit, commissioned in 1926. Rising from its perch atop a bluff, the 67-foot tower stood alongside a sturdy palm that rose to nearly the same altitude. This was the brightest beacon in Southern California, she'd read, and could be seen 20 miles at sea.

That painter Miranda Jones seemed to be following the trail of lighthouses too, though at a much slower pace than what she'd have to undertake herself. Jones created postcards of her beautiful watercolors, then had her Milford-Haven gallery sell them packaged with lighthouse stamps she apparently collected. The US Post Office did offer lovely collections of stamps, but they were published cyclically, so the artist must have bought out a few local sources in order to supply her followers with what she considered to be the best match for her small pieces of collectible art. Chris would make a point of stopping by to gather a few of these, then have her cameraman shoot some close-ups for her upcoming series. Now that would appeal to general audiences and collectors alike.

It was nearly midnight when Chris's SUV traced down the 405 past LAX until she found the turnoff onto the 107. Now she wound along Hawthorne through Rolling Hills Estates through increasingly exclusive neighborhoods of Pacific Palisades. This part of the city seemed to be a respite from the urban sprawl that'd taken over much of greater Los Angeles. She got glimpses of the opulent homes discretely stacked on the green hillsides overlooking the Pacific, wishing she could see this beautiful area by daylight *What would it be like to live here?* Joseph Calvin could afford it, but he already had a gorgeous ocean-view property. Her own budget couldn't touch this real estate with a ten foot contract.

She rolled onto the Point Vicente property where the strafe of the lighthouse reached her suddenly, bringing a sharp inhalation and a smile. There it stood, a reassuring presence. She pulled into the deserted parking lot, turned off the motor and stepped outside to breathe in the tang of ocean air. Shuddering in the sudden chill, she pulled a jacket from her front passenger seat, then grabbed her slim cross-body purse that held her pen and small notebook.

She closed her car door and locked the vehicle, though she doubted anyone would be along to break into it. Once again, she was surprised to find the visitor's office open, but when she entered, she evidently activated a sensor, because a dim overhead light illuminated.

On top of the counter she found the now familiar display of ink pad, scratch paper, and dated lighthouse stamp. She opened her purse to withdraw her notebook, flipping it open to the next blank page where she carefully added the new stamp.

Within the now illuminated case she again found historical artifacts: drawings, charts, daguerreotypes, and carefully printed legends describing what each of them was. And there a small booklet rested there too, titled "Lady of the Light: the Ghost Who Haunted the Point Vicente Light."

Chris left the building and began walking toward the lighthouse itself, glancing up at the bright windows at the top where she thought she saw a shadow moving across a pane. *The lamp itself casts shadows,* she thought.

She approached the open doorway at its base, a dark maw that both alarmed and beckoned. She entered and began the long climb to the top, counting out the seventy-four steps. As she approached the top, the darkness receded until she found herself standing in the very room where the active Fresnel blasted light across both land and water, a sparkling jewel of such immensity and power that she had to partially shield her eyes.

From the far side of the small, circular room nearly filled to capacity by the circulating lamp, she heard a rustling, then a woman's voice. "Beautiful, isn't it?"

"Oh!" Chris exclaimed. "You . . . I didn't realize anyone else was here!"

"I am. I'm always here on Veterans Day. Why are you?"

"Is this Veterans . . . um, why? Well, because I do research. I mean, I'm researching lighthouses."

"You're that journalist."

"I . . . you . . . I guess you've seen my broadcasts," Chris added, unsure whether to be flattered or alarmed this stranger knew who she was.

"Dangerous work."

"Well, I suppose it can be." Chris felt herself shudder at the memory of having fallen into that hole at the Clarke house. "But not usually."

"Dangerous," the woman repeated, "like my husband's job. Only he didn't have a choice."

"Your husband?" Chris asked.

"Never came home. Veterans are supposed to come home, that's why we celebrate them."

"I . . . I'm sorry for your loss," Chris said, beginning to think the woman might be unhinged. What was she really doing here? Performing some sort of personal ritual in honor of her dead husband?

"They're symbols of warning, you know," the woman said, still standing on the far side of the Fresnel.

"Sorry?"

"That's what lighthouses are."

"Uh-huh," Chris said, beginning to edge down the spiral staircase. It felt urgent, now, to descend, to depart. Her footsteps rang out on the metal steps as she clambered down, clinging to the railing lest she stumble.

When she reached the bottom, she burst out into the cool night air, relieved to be away from the claustrophobic confines of the light tower. She glanced up, and saw the silhouette of the woman evidently still standing in the lamp casement.

Then a thought touched her, like a cold, clammy hand. *What if that's her? The Lady of the Light? If that's her, then I just met a ghost.*

Chris couldn't seem to leave the Point Vicente grounds quickly enough, retracing her route back to the northbound freeway. Once she'd joined the light traffic traveling along the 405, she felt she'd put a safe distance between herself and that poor, strange woman she'd encountered at Point Vicente. Why did the woman feel she had to stay there? *She might be quite mad, still waiting the return of her war-hero husband who was never coming home.*

Perhaps that woman was actually both homeless and deranged, and had found she could squat at the lighthouse during the hours when no one else was there to monitor the facility.

One of the sad facts she'd discovered about the L.A. of the mid-1990s was that the homeless population had swelled, but no one knew exactly by how much. Her nearly photographic memory recalled a report she'd copied in the library and added to her files:

> In 1996, the City of Los Angeles Census 2000 Technical Committee began to evaluate the U.S. Census Bureau's methodology for counting homeless people.... At that time, the Bureau proposed to count homeless people living in shelters and soup kitchens or in encampments with 15 or more people. There were no provisions to count other homeless persons, such as individuals in streets and alleys or street groups in small encampments. Due to climate conditions in Los Angeles and the large physical size (467 square miles) of the City, the likelihood that most homeless people would be in shelters on the night of an official census count was very low.

The issue had been further compounded by the a recession, where thousands lost their jobs, and by the expelling of many patients from mental health facilities. This caused at least three groups to merge: the newly unemployed, the indigent and the mentally ill. *That should be another follow-up story. I'll pitch it next time I meet with the powers that be.*

Leaving that topic, she began to review the themes she might bring out in this future video essay on lighthouses. They stood as warnings, the stranger had said. Crazy though the woman might be, still her statement rang true. And the thing about warnings? Sometimes they were heeded, sometimes not. She herself had ignored her own internal alarms about going to that meeting at the Clarke house, hadn't she? And something bad had indeed happened. She'd taken a nasty fall and was lucky to have gotten out. She'd remember that in the future, take more notice when her intuition started flashing like a beacon.

So this warning would be one of the themes to highlight in her piece. What had she learned at Piedras Blancas? She thought back to the fog swirling through the grounds, the cryptic message on that note she'd found: "Things are not always as they seem."

Surely that was an accurate statement when it came to treacherous coastlines and the submerged rocks they concealed, the unexpectedly strong currents that swirled around promontories that might appear short at the surface, but were lengthy under water. So this, too, was a good theme to mention, and to exemplify with the right footage and supporting historical mentions. She'd learned lighthouses were almost always connected to maritime disasters, perhaps because mariners couldn't see the dangers in the waters they plied, and ventured too close to shore thinking they'd be safe.

Then she thought back to the lighthouse lady, still spooked at the idea she was a ghost haunting the light, but more convinced, now, the poor woman had been driven mad over the loss of her husband.

What would it be like to love someone, literally, to distraction? Is that the goal? Romantic love bordering on obsession? She might've experienced something like that once, but so long ago that she scarecely remembered. Her high school sweetheart. People did marry those early loves sometimes. And sometimes it even worked. But she and Ron had too many obstacles too young. Chris had learned to harden her heart and make her own way, rather than leave herself so vulnerable.

Where had vulnerability ever gotten her? That awkward episode at Joseph's party was a case in point. The remembrance shot through her like a nasty electric shock, the shame and humiliation bringing first heat, and then a dreadful, aching cold that seemed to settle in her bones. Why couldn't he just have been honest with her? Why parade his attentions to another woman in front of her, ignore her in front of his other guests, even seem to pretend he hadn't seen her standing there?

"Men!" She shouted into the car. "Can't live with 'em, can't live without 'em!" Although, she had done just that most of her adult life. Living without them had worked well for her career-focused life. Only lately had she realized some sort of longing had begun to rear its head. Family . . . children . . . those had never been her dreams. But companionship with someone smart and kind, someone whose company she could stand, and who could stand hers . . . that had always been a goal, one she'd come close to hitting a few times, but "close" didn't count when it came to finding a mate.

Is this part of the warning? Not to love too much, too deeply? Not to risk obsession, desperation, dysfunction? Maybe she should read the little booklet about the Lady of the Light to see who she really was, and what fate had actually befallen her. On the other hand, Chris decided she didn't really want to know.

Chapter 9

Delmar spent a lot of time on the road. Since his was a county job, he was expected to travel to whatever part of the 3,616 square miles needed his attention. Indeed, sometimes his work took him south into Santa Barbara County, or even farther afield. He went where his cases led.

All the driving past unfamiliar landmarks had piqued his curiosity and he now knew quite a bit about his territory. The Salinas River flowed north-northwest through the Central Coast region of the state and emptied into Monterey Bay. Along the way, it delivered vital water to ranches and vineyards, farms, towns, and two military bases. And the Santa Maria River served as the southern border of the county.

Small, oddly shaped mountains dotted the landscape, beginning with the distinctive Morro Rock, plunked down like a Moorish hat, for which it was named, in the middle of its namesake bay. These turned out to be the 22-million-year-old Nine Sisters, a volcanic field in the Santa Lucia Range—volcanic plugs of magma that'd solidified inside softer rock long since eroded away.

A chain of mountains formed a cordillera: Morro Rock was first at 576 feet, then Black Hill, Cerro Cabrillo, Hollister Peak, Cerro Romauldo, Chumash Peak, Bishop Peak, Cerro San Luis, and Islay Hill, ranging in altitude between about 200 to 1,500 feet. Hollister was one of the most impressive, and he wished its hiking trail were still accessible, but the property was private, now, where once it'd been a sacred mountain to the Chumash.

Nestled in the middle of the county was San Luis Obispo, a gem of a town, listed as one of the best places to live in the U.S., with its historic downtown, temperate weather and sense of community.

He liked the college-town atmosphere provided by students at Cal Poly and Cuesta, that youthful energy that swirled through campuses fueled by scientific and artistic studies. Yet even with a wide range of offerings to students, the county was still 70 percent Caucasian, 20 percent Latino, 4 percent Asian, and 2 percent African-American. There was no question that Del stood out in this county, unable to blend in as he could in L.A.

During his first few months, he'd rented an efficiency unit in SLO. With department headquarters located there, this seemed to make sense, and it meant Del also had a straight shot on highway 101 to the northern office in Templeton.

But the unincorporated towns in the county that stretched along a hundred miles of coastline had no local police and depended solely on the sheriffs for law enforcement, which sometimes left the populace underserved. The sheriffs had made arrangements to have a north coast office in Milford-Haven, courtesy of the Department of Forestry, and the room in the shared space had become Del's official office.

That being the case, Del had contacted a local agency for help locating a long-term rental. They'd found him a cozy single-family house that he now regarded more and more as home. Perched atop a hill overlooking Highway 1 and the ocean beyond, he had both immediate access to the road he so frequently had to travel, and the quiet privacy of a small town. Like the other houses on the block, his was surrounded by tall pines, and through their branches he had a partial view of the Pacific from his second floor bedroom.

And now that he worked in the Milford-Haven office, he was more glad than ever not to have to drive more than five minutes when he left work—especially when he left late, as he often did.

Tonight was a case in point. During regular office hours, he'd spent some more time researching Clarke Shipping in Morro Bay, in whose offices he'd previously met with two women. One was Gladys Washington, a rock-solid citizen who worked there by day, but who also volunteered at Safe Haven, a local women's shelter. Not only did he admire her community spirit, he felt a special kinship as she was one of the few fellow African-Americans living and working along this stretch of the coast.

The other was Stacey Chernak, a jittery, perplexing European transplant who showed every sign of being in an abusive relationship. Until she chose to report the abuse, there was nothing he could do officially, but keep an eye on her.

With that, and socializing with Gladys as excuses, he also found he had a good cover to check further into the operations at Clarke Shipping. He'd discovered a connection to Calvin Oil; it made sense that a Santa Barbara oil company would have a professional relationship with a local shipping firm. But he'd also discovered that Stacey's husband, Wilhelm Chernak, had a connection of his own to Clarke Shipping, which didn't quite make sense. Why would the husband of Stacey, a secretary at the firm, also be doing business with them at some higher level? Armed with a few more factoids, he promised himself he'd drop by to visit Gladys soon, then hang around long enough to check on Stacey.

Before leaving the office this evening he wanted to take another look at Chris Christian's notebook. He kept it with him these days, in case he wanted to check dates or references, and he pulled it from his work satchel.

Not that I'm eager to read the journal of a dead woman. Presumed dead, he corrected himself, still hoping it wasn't so.

Lifting it, he ran his hands over the smooth, black leatherette perfect-bound book. Not an expensive item—she hadn't chosen real leather or linen for her work book. Yet it had a simple elegance—classy, understated, functional. He asked himself for the hundredth time whether or not he had the right to read someone else's private writings.

Again, without reading the pages in sequence, he opened it at random a few times, finding the Piedras Blancas stamp, where he hesitated. Then, turning to a few pages later, he found another lighthouse stamp.

Surprised, he brought the book closer to examine the image. *Must've missed this last time I looked.* Block letters clearly printed surrounded the edge of an elongated oval: POINT VICENTE LIGHTHOUSE-LOS ANGELES, CA. In the center stood a tall tower. Where the Piedras structure angled out toward its base, this one stood perfectly straight. Though slightly smudged, the stamp showed a darkened chamber at its top and he could see the faint outline of a window.

Once again, next to the lighthouse stamp, there was a circular date stamp: November 11, 1996. *Last autumn. So she went there just a couple of weeks after she visited Piedras. That's gotta mean she was working on a story. Wonder if I'll unearth a file folder with notes at some point.*

Of course, since these visits of hers would have been for a future story, these stamps in her notebook had no bearing on the videos he'd be reviewing. But it was interesting to consider both where her career had led her previously, and where it was leading her next. Indeed, these date stamps could be vital clues to discovering where she'd gone, and where she might be now . . . dead or alive.

If she's still alive, taking time off, time away, what right do I have to be reading her personal notes? But if she's trying to outrun something or someone, maybe I really do have the right.

Of course, he could rationalize that it was his job to read her notes. Yet it surprised him what hesitance he felt. But if, by reading its pages, he could find her . . . hear her through the mist of time and circumstance . . . help her, or help her rest if indeed her spirit wandered . . . then, his eyes on her words and images might be the most important part of his job.

Chris sighed with relief when she saw the turn-off that would take her off the 405 north. Were she continuing in that direction, the next freeway sign she'd have seen would be to the 101 south—though in the San Fernando Valley the 101 actually traveled west to east.

She laughed out loud at the inherent confusion in these designations, remembering how perplexed she'd felt when she first moved to Los Angeles from New York. In 1980, so many assignments had taken her to the west coast that she'd stopped putting her suitcase away, always leaving it partially packed. Finally, she'd given up the fight, admitted to herself that her destiny lay on the other coast, and sold her New York co-op. The nice chunk of money had allowed her to buy a place near L.A.'s famous Farmer's Market, a neighborhood with as much resemblance to NYC as she could find. With her own multi-cultural background, a Russian deli, an Israeli hardware store, an upscale Chinese restaurant, an Argentine car repair shop, and a French laundry had all helped make her feel comfortable.

And then she found a building she loved. Built in 1937 with three two-story units, it had its own garden, a garage in back, and a set of features that'd probably been designed for movie starlets of a bygone era.

By the time Chris had scraped off old paint, torn out shag carpet, had the hard wood floors redone and given all the rooms a fresh coat of paint, she adored it, possibly even more than she'd loved her New York apartment.

As though drawn by the memory, she headed there now, visualizing unlocking the back door, dropping her bag, stepping out of her shoes, and then sliding between the cool sheets she knew awaited.

Yet when she arrived, she couldn't locate the garage door opener. She parked on the street and headed for the front door, but as she approached, she noticed the place looked different, somehow. And then, with a jolt, she remembered. *I don't live here any more. I moved to Santa Maria!*

Leaping back into her car, she sped through the empty streets back toward the freeway. *I must have really been rattled by that lady at the lighthouse,* she thought, the adrenaline rush beginning to ebb.

She felt as though she were forgetting something . . . an appointment of some kind, probably to interview someone. The northern suburbs of L.A. slipped past her in the night, and she couldn't very well look at her day planner while traveling 65 miles an hour.

Calmer now, she thought back to the lady in the lighthouse, and also to the strange circumstance of finding the gate open at night, both there, and at Piedras Blancas. Were squatters getting into these properties at night? No one monitored them after hours. Should she report this to someone?

Yes . . . that made sense. She'd seen the SLO County medallion on the side of the SUV she'd passed the other day. She knew the offices in San Luis Obispo would be closed at this hour. *Would any office be open now?*

Engrossed in her thoughts, she hadn't paid attention to the route she knew so well, nor particularly to the time of day, but evidently the sun had risen above a gray cloud cover. She glanced left, noticing the Morro Bay power plant with its three distinctive stacks rising 450 feet against the hard, bright flash of light on a metallic bay.

A formation of fog began to drape itself across the hills up ahead, as though a huge sea lion napped on the ridge. But as she drew closer, the temperature plummeted and the lumens dimmed. Twilight seemed to fall, as wraithlike tendrils of fog rose like whiskers of the beast tickling the underbelly of the clouds. The sun, rather than making a gradual orange descent, sank as rapidly as an approaching eclipse and the landscape shifted into night.

She'd been about to pull to the side of the road for lack of visibility, when she suddenly emerged on Main Street in Milford-

Haven. Though the town appeared shuttered for the night, she saw light shining from a window in a large redwood building.

Chris parked, grabbed her purse, and headed toward a sign posted beside the front door. "California Department of Forestry," it read, and under that, "SLO County Sheriff's Department, North Coast Office."

"I knew I'd find the right place," she said aloud. And then she walked inside.

Chapter 10

Del had closed down his computer for the day, put away his files, and stepped out for a quick dinner at the Bird's Nest. By now, he was used to the powder blue walls, the small wicker baskets full of antique silver-plated flatware on the tables, and the few but excellent offerings. Tonight he craved a big bowl of *bouillabaisse*, which was delivered piping hot, along with some steamed fresh rolls. Then, armed with a huge coffee-to-go, he'd headed back to the conference room he was allowed to share at the Forestry building.

Retrieving his stash of videos, he glanced at the sticky-note he'd affixed to the top cassette: "Wish I could review these with Chris." The small note reminded him how many questions he had for this woman, should he ever find her.

He loaded Tape 2 into the VCR and the screen illuminated in its now familiar royal blue. But before hitting "Play," he braced himself. When he'd watched the first tape, the shock of seeing her had slapped him. There she'd been, moving across the screen as if here in the room with him.

Why do I feel such a personal connection with the missing woman? Hers was, after all, designated as a cold case, one with no leads, that captured no one else's interest. Its file lay stacked with the others in the Special Projects Unit archive. But to him the case was personal. Something about it felt important, though he had yet to figure out what, or why. He only knew he had to trust his gut, as he always did. And his gut told him to keep digging.

So, here he was, almost feeling as though he were flirting with a woman he'd never met. Once again a piece of advice from his mother came to mind. "When those unexplainable things pop up, don't ignore them, son. They're the Guidance. Someone's there to help you, even if you can't see them."

Not even an entire adult life in the City of the Angels had been able to filter the Bayou Wisdom out of his mother, the daughter of a New Orleans native. A devout Christian, she'd still held to the birth gift she said came from her ancestors. The Celts called it Second Sight. In the Bayou, they called it conjuration. His grandmother Sapphire, and to some extent his mother Ruby—all the women in the family having been named for jewels—had the ability to commune with what they called spirits.

Del dismissed these ancient family practices as out of date and uneducated. He remembered the sharp embarrassment he'd felt in childhood when his grandmother offered a super-natural explanation for some event. He'd then work all the harder to find a logical one. *She's probably the reason I'm a detective, he reflected. I had to prove her wrong.*

Though he'd never admitted it to his Granny Sparkle Blue— his own childhood name for her—there truly were unexplained things in the universe, and he'd learned to live with that fact. Sometimes intuition made a leap across synapses that logic could never follow, or a startling synergy would bring together two elements that solved a difficult case. Colleagues called it luck. He called it Granny Wisdom.

He knew these thoughts were surfacing now, in this dark-ened room, because something remained unexplained about the Chris Christian case and his connection to it.

Last week he'd forced himself to watch that first tape a second time. He'd watched it again to steady himself, he admitted, to regain his objectivity, check for details from which her on-camera charisma might have distracted him. He hoped he'd see something —or someone—in the background of a shot that would give him a hint or a clue to follow. Even something out of place might give him a starting point.

Now, as he readied to watch the second segment of her report, he forced himself through another process, that of recognition. Of course he'd never met her. But a) did she remind him of someone he did know? If so, he'd have to carefully discount memories associated with that person, lest they contaminate his work on the case. And b) had he seen her before?

He'd tackle "a" first. Though he'd attended an inner-city school, it didn't happen often that a boy growing up in South Central befriended a white girl, let alone an aloof blonde with patrician bearing and effortless grace.

But what would Chris have looked like as a kid? Gangly, rather than graceful? Probably. Shy rather than self-assured? He smiled at the prospect, then laughed out loud at the imagined scenario of meeting her then: he, a 14-year-old kid too tall for his clothes focused only on one thing: basketball; and her, a 16-year-old girl trying to be cool and stay out of trouble, petrified to offend the members of the girl-clique, and even more afraid to talk to boys in the hallway, let alone a younger one, let alone a black one.

And then it struck him. He *did* remember a girl like that from Compton High. Had she been a friend of R's? The boy two years his senior had "joined" the family while his mother dated a man neither he nor his sister ever liked. Del's temporary "brother" had insisted on being called "R." And when their respective parents had gone their separate ways, they'd never kept in touch. Delmar's nuclear family had been close and better off without the intruders.

Los Angeles was nothing if not a multi-cultural city, though neighborhoods and schools tended to be segregated, despite the L.A. Unified School Districts goal to actually "unify" students. Thanks to a 1961 law suit, students did have the right to attend the school closest to their homes, but with white, black, and especially Hispanic groups tending to live in familiar surroundings, schools were predominantly one race or another.

Who was that girl? He remembered hearing that she lived with her family in Gardena, on the other side of the freeway. It'd been the 1960s, and they'd been caught in that transition from white to black. Now, it was mostly Hispanic.. *But then . . . we were black kids were suddenly moving in on the whites. Anyway, I'm way off topic, now. Focus, man!*

Del shook his head as though to rid himself of his musings, and hit Play. When Chris Christian's image appeared once again on the screen, he muttered, "Nice of you to show up for our date."

Chris had entered the building and headed midway down a long corridor where light spilled out. When she saw a stack of video cassette tapes on a long conference table, she looked over her shoulder, then stepped closer. The sticky-note she found there made her smile. *Great minds.* This guy with the sheriff's department might value her work, and maybe even her report. He must be here somewhere. *But I should knock, or something, rather than be discovered already in this room.*

She decided to avail herself of the restroom she found farther down the hallway. When she returned, so had he, and she watched as he put one of the tapes into the VCR player, then heard what he said, "Nice of you to show up for our date."

She was confused for a moment. *What does he mean by date?* In as polite a tone as she could muster, she said, "Uh . . . sorry. Am I late?"

"Not really a date. An appointment, let's say," Del added.

"Oh. Right." Chris looked down the length of the large, sturdy table, its surface pock-marked with white rings left by mugs or glasses. Marching along its sides was a collection of worn leather swivel chairs. She sat in one and it squeaked slightly.

Del glanced in her direction, but then quickly returned his gaze to the screen.

Into the awkward silence she said, "So . . . looks like you already reviewed the first episode in the series and you're at the end of episode two."

"I better watch this again."

"Really? I'm flattered." Chris felt a warm flush heat her face.

"Blond hair, tan blazer, white blouse, black slacks. Flawless on-camera makeup," Del catalogued. "Professional appearance and calm demeanor inspires confidence, as does speaking with authority."

"Wow," Chris remarked. "Are you looking for a producing job?"

Del hit the pause button, looked down and ran a hand over his hair. Chris wasn't sure whether to ask him if everything was all right, but then he hit "Play" again, so she let it go.

Since Del made no further comment and became completely absorbed in segment two of her adoption story, Chris decided she'd rather not watch again the footage she'd spent weeks reviewing and editing. *He won't miss me if I'm gone for a couple of minutes.* She stood, stepped into the corridor and went looking for the break room she imagined must be nearby. *Maybe I can grab a coffee.*

Sure enough, the break room featured a simple kitchenette complete with a hot water dispenser and containers of powdered concoctions. *International Italian Cappuccino* caught her eye—a small rectangular tin with a plastic snap-on lid, which she pulled off. Finding utensils in a drawer, she placed a few heaping tea-spoons in a large Styrofoam cup and filled it to the brim with the boiling water.

"Well, it smells good enough," she said aloud. "And it'll be warm." By the time she returned to her chair in the conference room, Del had started on Segment three. *He must've fast-forwarded through the rest of Segment two. I can't even imagine any more how this series would look to a fresh pair of eyes.* Chris took the trusty notebook from her purse and began jotting down a few random notes.

"Looking down a bit too much in this section. I don't
have to look at camera all the time, but I could look
around as if noticing details in the surroundings instead of looking at my shoes."

Always her own worst critic, nonetheless she did believe she
could always do better, and nothing provided the proof better than
the on-air shows she'd recorded, produced and reviewed over
the years. *Best way to keep my edge.*

Del stood and left the room, running a hand over his face as
he passed her. Chris watched him go. *Not a talkative type. Heading
for the rest room, I guess. Or maybe I inspired him to get his own
coffee.*

Sure enough, a few moments later, he came back in with a
steaming cup, set it down by his place, and hit "Play" for segment
three.

Chris sighed, embarrassed and confused at being ignored. At
this point she wasn't sure why he'd jotted that note. *Did he think
I needed to see the footage again in order to discuss it with him?*

The video on the screen grabbed her attention. What she
did love was seeing Dr. Swain on the screen, one of her favorite
interview subjects in this, or maybe any other, series. Dr. Sheila
Swain, PhD.—formerly Dean of Students at Coronado Community
College, and now founder of the non-profit Present Parents—had
captured not only Chris's attention, but also her undying respect.

Her voice husky with emotion held in check, her diction
flawless and dignified, Dr. Swain continued. "Therefore, the only
father-figures young black children grew up with were the local
preachers, and it was the churches that became the centers of the
community. It was in the churches that families got everything
from a reason to dress right, to a good square meal."

Del gulped, evidently wrestling with an emotional reaction.
He seemed to be talking to himself when he said, "This woman
could be telling my story. She could be my mother. Or, in another
life, this is what my mother could've become, were it not for having
to raise me." Then he put his head down on the conference table.

Is he . . . crying? Chris sat as still as she could in her chair, willing herself not to remind him he had an audience. He made no further sound, and she thought he must be deep in thought, but then she began to wonder whether he was drifting off.

Now what do I do? Stay here and let him sleep? He'll be embarrassed when he wakes. Say something right now? Excuse myself? Feeling her best recourse would be just to ask. She cleared her throat and said, "Would you like me to stay?"

Del woke with such a start that he bolted upright from his chair, catapulting it backward on its rollers until it smacked into the wall with a resounding boom.

"Oh!" Chris exclaimed.

"Jesus H!" Del cried.

"Sorry, I—"

"Didn't realize you were—"

"Still here? Well, you did say you wished you could review the tapes with me."

Del felt the adrenaline begin to drain, his heartbeat slowing. "Right. I did. Wish that you could. Okay. Great. This is great."

Chris gave him a tentative smile. "Um, shall we sit?"

"Sit? Yes! Yes, have a seat. You want . . . I see you have coffee.

"Such as it is. "

"You know. Cop coffee."

Both of them laughed, which pulled at least half the tension from the room. They sat, their chairs squeaking.

Del ran a hand over his hair, then over his face. "I have . . . I have so many questions. Not sure where to start."

Confused, Chris asked, "About adoption?"

"No! No," he countered. "It's a great series. I know more than I ever thought I would. Actually, your series could help me with another case. You're good at what you do. Great, in fact."

Chris found his praise inordinately reassuring. Touched and suddenly shy, she said, "Th . . . thanks. That means a lot. I like the digging, you know? The investigating, peeling back the layers."

"Exactly!" Del leaned in, his forearms on the table. "That's what I like, what drew me to this career."

"Same here. Well, not the same career, but there are similarities I guess."

Del nodded. "More than I realized. So . . . okay . . . the most obvious question is, where have you been?"

Dismissively, Chris replied, "I got caught up in a story I was researching."

"Yeah, but where? I mean, people have been worried. I've been worried."

Now it was Chris's turn to lean toward the table. "You? Oh! You don't mean the Sheriff's Department. . . ."

"Not officially. No evidence of foul play. Your boss says you disappear for long stretches when you travel on assignments. But . . ." He inhaled, exhaled. "I'm glad you're safe. A lot of other folks will be too."

"I didn't mean to worry anyone. I just . . . when I got that call to go to the Clarke house, I just knew I could finally get the lead I'd been looking for."

Del seemed about ready to jump out of his skin. "The Clarke house? The unfinished one?" His voice rose. "You went there? Why?"

"Okay," she said, using a calming tone. "It's complicated," she admitted. "The Clarke house is owned by Russell Clarke, who owns Clarke Shipping. They've got an office in Morro Bay."

Del looked around, then stood to grab a pen and pad of paper from the built-in table at the side of the room. "Right," he confirmed, jotting notes. "Been there."

Chris peered at Del's bent head, his quick strokes of the pen. *This is someone who could become a trusted source, a colleague of sorts . . . maybe even a friend. I've never really been able to discuss this investigation with anyone before.* "So I've been doing deep background on the oil business for months. Make that years." She laughed without humor. "The deeper I delve, the more ambivalent I feel, and it's hard to keep objective. I mean, we need the oil, but we're not really tracking the cost."

Del looked up at her and asked, "How does Joseph Calvin fit in?"

She felt herself inhale sharply. *This guy doesn't pull any punches.* "That . . . that got complicated. I started dating him. Talk about losing objectivity. I was either going to have to recuse myself from looking into Calvin Oil, or terminate my relationship with him . . . although, that now seems to be a moot point."

A sudden awkwardness cooled the excitement that'd seemed to warm them both a moment earlier.

Del broke the silence. "Let's come back to that. Tell me about Clarke Shipping and Calvin Oil."

"Right," she said, wishing, now, she had some of her files with her. "They do business together, which makes sense: off-shore rigs need tankers, and vice versa. But something came up about missing persons—not tied to Calvin Oil, but to Clarke Shipping. So that was one thing I flagged."

"Ha. Really?"

"Then there was something else," she went on. "Some government experiment. It started toward the end of WWII. Clarke was involved. And so was another man who now lives in Morro Bay. His wife works at Clarke Shipping."

"Stacey Chernak," Del stated.

"Yes! You know about her?!"

Chris stared into his dark eyes, and he held her gaze just as steadily. If the room had felt electrified before, now it felt like a live wire sizzled between them across the table.

He knows most of what I know. He's been following the same threads.

Del cleared his throat. "I don't know much about Mrs. Chernak. I know she's in a domestic nightmare."

"Interesting. Not surprising, I suppose, given the likely character of her husband." She paused, looked down at her hands, then up again into those eyes. "We should . . . I've got stacks of notes, notebooks full of dangling ends." Using the metaphor that'd come to her a moment earlier, she added, "They're like live wires that keep zapping me until I can make the connections."

"Hmm," Del considered. "Sounds like you've got more pieces of the puzzle than I do, but I think I could help."

"This is . . . well, it's amazing. I didn't think I had nearly enough to interest someone in law enforcement."

And then he warmed the room again with a smile that went right through her. "Well, you've got my interest." He returned her gaze for a moment, as though sharing a deep understanding. Then he said, "So . . . talk about a dangling thread. You go to the Clarke house. Then what?"

Chris leaned back in her chair, replaying that evening in her mind. "My contact is a no-show. I walk around the house. It's dark, kind of spooky. I wait for a while. I mean, this guy promised key information, so I didn't want to miss him. And then I fell."

"Fell?"

A shudder shook through her. "There was a hole in front of the fireplace, where the hearth will go. Didn't see it in the dark. I fell, hit my head. I've still got a nasty bump." She felt for it, then dropped her hand in her lap. "I have no idea how long I was down there. I woke up in the pitch black, felt my way till I found stairs, climbed out."

Del's expression was both sympathetic and horrified, and he slowly nodded his head, as though he were picturing the scene. "You said there was a hole when you fell, so, no stairs. But then when you climbed out, there were stairs?"

Chris thought for a moment. "Yeah. That doesn't quite make sense. Unless I just didn't notice them when I fell. I mean, I could have fallen from the other side of the opening."

"Mm-hmm," he agreed. But then he asked, "Any chance you had help with that fall?"

"Help?"

"I'm saying . . . is it possible someone pushed you?"

"I . . . there's . . ." Chris began to shudder again. "Honestly, I can't quite remember. I've had some trouble, lately, since that head injury. There are some gaps."

An expression of alarm now began to take over Del's face. Chris laughed nervously, her teeth almost chattering. "At least . . . I finally . . . got out of there alive."

Very quietly, Del replied, "Chris, I'm not sure you did."

Confused, she said, "Did what?"

His eyes filled with concern or compassion. He said, "Get out of there alive."

Chapter 11

D el startled awake in the conference room, jerking his head up
off the table so quickly he felt dizzy.

"Holy Fuck," he said out loud, using words to scare away
whatever apparition might still be lurking on the premises. For
the second time tonight—or was it the first?—his heart raced
and his hands shook.

"It's okay," he said aloud, trying to steady his breathing. "She's
not here. It was a dream."

He figured if he ever needed bright lights and coffee, this
would be the moment. He flipped on the overheads on his way
down the hall to the break room, using every bit of his macho
pride not to peer into each door along the way.

Once back to his chair with his refilled Styrofoam cup, he
took a sip, but set it aside as no longer worth drinking. He sat
still for a moment, inhaling the faint trace of... what? *I know that
scent. Is it what Granny Sparkle wore?* The more he tried to identify it the more it faded, so he let it go and reached for his notepad,
finding it already open, with a few previously jotted notes. *I don't
remember writing anything down tonight.* Ignoring the concern

that raised, he focused instead to see whether he could remember everything the dream had contained.

"Connection between Wilhelm Chernak and Clarke Shipping," he scribbled. _What else?_ "Not surprised to learn Stacey Chernak is likely being abused."

It was so damn real! He wanted to rush to his captain to share the new clues and leads. _But... based on what evidence?_ He wanted to charge over to that abuser Chernak's home and cart him off in hand cuffs. _I'd end up in jail, instead of him._ Del just wanted to tell someone—anyone—about this. But who?

The answer rose from whatever corner of his mind where he'd been holding it down, trying to keep it from surfacing, like trying to keep a beach ball under water.

Tanzi. That's who I have to call.

But first, he better get his facts in order. Because if this was what he thought it might be . . . if this was "the Guidance," as his Granny Sparkle Blue would say . . . then it would rock his world, and maybe his sister's, too.

Del decided he wanted to make this call from his home, not this conference room, where the dream had taken place.

He locked up and drove the short distance to his house. After stowing his weapon, he poured himself the last of the coffee left in this morning's thermos, but added a one-finger pour of bourbon. Then he settled at his kitchen table, his pad and pencil ready in case he wanted to take notes.

He went over what he'd say to his sister. As usual, it'd been too long since he'd called, so he'd have to make his excuses, knowing she wouldn't believe them, but letting him off the hook.

But Tanzi was nobody's fool. In a matter of seconds, she'd probably sense he had a purpose for calling, beyond the customary check-in, and on the matter of his true motive, she would not be letting him off the hook. By the time he placed the call, he knew it'd be late in Atlanta. He also knew his sister was a night owl, and her husband wasn't, so their conversation stood a better chance of being private. He sighed, knowing he needed both information and wise counsel from her.

He dialed, and was surprised when his sister picked up on the second ring. Slightly breathless, his sister's voice said, "Hello-u." Tanzi and Rahn had moved to Atlanta years earlier, and it seemed to Del that each time they spoke, her accent was a little thicker. *The better to fit in, I suppose.*

"Hey, Sis."

"You okay?"

Del winced, realizing her first thought was that he was hurt. Now he knew it'd really been too long since his last call.

"Fine! Yes," he reassured.

"Whew. Glad to know it."

"How's it going?"

There followed a recitation of his nephews' sports events, Rahn's business successes, and her latest community award. "I could keep goin' and talk about my last manicure. Should I? Or do you have something to say?"

Oh, Jesus, that therapist thing has kicked in and she already knows I need to ask her something. How does she do that? Why do I have all these intuitive women in my life?

"I am okay," he began. "But I had an interesting experience."

"Well, that doesn't sound good," she remarked.

"It's complicated," he admitted.

"Oh, Lord. You've got someone pregnant and she's still married."

"No!" Del wailed. "It's nothing like that!"

"Mm-hum."

"Tanzi, this is a work thing, not a personal one. I mean . . . it's personal, but related to work."

His sister paused, then asked, "Don't you have regulations about not dating people at work?"

"We're not dating. In fact, she might be dead," he blurted.

He heard a sharp inhale through the phone. "What in the world does that mean?"

Del took a sip of his now cold, spiked coffee, then almost whispered, "You can't discuss this with anyone."

"If you're gonna divulge info about a case, you better think twice, Delmar. I don't want to participate in you gettin' yourself in trouble."

"No, I won't be giving you enough detail for that." Del sighed. "There's been a cold case on the books for a few months now, missing person."

"Oh, mercy, those are awful."

"Yeah," he confirmed. "She does travel a lot for her work, and she still might be on a trip somewhere, or maybe stuck in some foreign jail, or whatever, but I . . . I don't think so."

"And why is that?"

"I think I . . . I might've seen her, or something."

Delmar heard a door close on his sister's end of the phone. Then, in a quieter tone of voice, she asked, "Are you sayin' she's passed over and you can hear her?"

There it was, laid out in all its simplicity and complexity. "I've never believed, Tanzi."

"Well, that never stopped Granny Sparkle from doin' what she did or knowin' what she knew."

"No, it didn't."

"She always said you had the gift. And she said it likely wouldn't show up till later. This is later."

"Yeah," he confirmed.

"I don't know how much I can really help, little brother," her voice tender. "I don't have the gift myself."

"But you witnessed it a lot more than I did. I was either too much of dork or too busy with basketball."

His sister inhaled. "I did go with her for a few readings. This may sound strange, but there was nothin' weird about those sessions. It was like you'd have a meeting with your minister, or your counselor. For her, hearing those messages from the departed ones was just as normal as rain."

"Did she—" He began. "How did she know it was real? How did she tell them apart from dreams?" He heard the imploring note in his own voice.

"Well, they didn't come to her in dreams, Del. They just spoke right up and she could hear. But . . . hmm, I do remember her saying something about dreams. She said some folks could only hear them in their dreams."

The hair on the back of Del's neck stood up.

"She said for people who had the Gift come in the night dreams, that they should protect themselves," Tanzi continued.

"Protect . . . did she say how?" Del wanted to know.

"Bathe yourself in strength, and bathe the others in kindness," she would say. "They're frightened, so they act out sometimes."

They, he thought. *Like they're real. Well, Chris was real enough for me.* "Granny Sparkle just saw them, plain as she could see real people?" he asked.

"Delmar, our grandmother didn't make anything up," Tanzi said defensively.

"No, I—"

"She didn't ask for the Gift. But she did try to do her best with it."

"I know," Del soothed. "I know she did." His sister paused for a moment, and so did he.

"What exactly happened, Delmar?"

He sighed, settled back in his chair. "This case . . . this woman went missing. She was . . . is . . . a respected television journalist. I started reviewing videos of her broadcasts. Then I got . . . I don't know, tired or overwhelmed, or. . . . I put my head down on the table in the conference room at work, and next thing you know, she wakes me up, saying she's there to review the tapes with me. Like I'd invited her."

"And did you?" Tanzi asked.

"I suppose, in a way, I did."

"Okay, that's one of the things Granny Sparkle always did say. They'll come if they're invited."

The skin on Del's arms prickled.

"You're investigating her disappearance. Maybe she came to give you clues," Tanzi suggested. "If so, you can check them out, can't you?"

"Yes. That I can and will do."

Tanzi chuckled. "You'll know what to do, Delmar. I trust you. I think this missing woman does, too."

Chris woke up in her bed, shuddering and disoriented—again. At some point she'd evidently thrown her covers off, and as she sat up, realized she was chilled to the bone. She heard the splashing percussion of raindrops outside her window, and knew a storm must have moved in over night.

Rising, she ran a bath, adding a few drops of her favorite lavender oil, and slid into the heated water. She enjoyed soaking, then dried herself and pulled on fleece-lined sweats and wooly socks. *That warmed me up on the outside; tea will do it on the inside.* While the kettle heated, she flipped on her gas fireplace, then sat in her one comfy chair close by, and stuck her feet on the hearth.

As her chill subsided, she had the feeling something good had just happened, but couldn't remember what. The whistling kettle brought her back to the kitchen, and the remembrance to her mind. *That deputy! He listened to me!*

An enormous sense of relief flooded through her, and for the first time she realized how much anxiety she'd been holding—some vague sense that important work she'd done would be lost, and her mission left incomplete. Now she felt she had a colleague, someone who respected her research, believed her insights.

A warm mug of jasmine tea in hand, she headed for her home office, where she began reviewing the folders in the locked file cabinet where she kept only the most active projects. The one labeled "Chernak" had her notes on Wilhelm Chernak, originally from Switzerland, and a few European newspaper articles she'd managed to print from library microfiche. *Del will want these for sure.* She then jotted his name on a sticky-note, adding his own insight: *Stacey Chernak likely suffers domestic abuse from husband.*

That was a missing piece that just might make Mr. Chernak more vulnerable to prosecution—if someone like a sheriff's deputy was already watching his behavior.

Then she opened the file labeled "Mr. Man"—the only name she had for that elusive contact she was supposed to have met at the Clarke house, the one who never showed up. She'd had several phone conversations with him. She privately fantasized that she had her very own "Deep Throat," a well-connected source who provided information on condition he could remain anonymous. *All the more reason I was so eager to meet him in person, finally.*

She stacked these, and some other folders, on her desk, wondering how to transport them, and when she'd be able to get together again with Deputy Delmar Johnson. She'd read his name on the nameplate pinned over the breast pocket of his starched uniform shirt.

But I know him from somewhere. The familiarity had been there from the moment she'd seen his face flash by on the 101. If she was honest, she also remembered him from the party at Joseph's, though she'd been too shy to speak to him then.

He does look a little bit like Ron. Maybe that's it. That long ago high school friend. *Delmar probably looks something like Ron would look now.* But who knows? In any case, the most important thing is that now she had a real contact in law enforcement.

***

While still at her desk, Chris had also reviewed her lighthouse notes, and had begun to feel some urgency about visiting another one on the Central Coast.

Sometimes when considering a story from several angles, she tended to doodle in her notebook, so she wasn't completely surprised to look down and discover she'd sketched a sand dollar.

She'd looked up the species at one point, and she walked her fingers through her research file drawer until she found the folder labeled Sea Shells: Sand Dollar. Finding her notes, she read:

The "skeleton" is called a "test." They look much different when alive, and when dead. When dead, they're
bleached white, resembling silver on the sand, thus
the name sand dollar. When alive, they're covered
with short velvety spines that may be purple, reddish
brown, yellowish, gray, green or black.

Related to sea stars; basically a sea urchin. These are
called irregular echinoids, so they have a front, a back,
and basic bilateral symmetry on top.

The test is its endoskeleton, lying underneath the
spines and skin. The top (aboral) surface of the
test has a pattern that looks like five petals.
There are five sets of tube feet that extend from these
petals, which the sand dollar uses for respiration; this
is how they avoid suffocation.

Chris suddenly began experiencing a strange shortness of
breath, as though she herself might be suffocating. Inhaling deeply,
she put a hand on her chest and forced herself to calm down. *Ugh,
that was weird. I guess just the thought of not being able to breathe
got to me for a moment. So . . . why was I drawing a sand dollar?*

She considered the lighthouse visits she'd made so far,
sketching their locations roughly on a separate page of her notebook. She'd gone north to Piedras Blancas, then south to Point
Vicente; did that mean she should look for two more to represent
east and west? Was this a cardinal points thing, orienting herself
to the subject? She plotted two more lighthouses on her rough
map: Point San Luis and Point Conception, both of which were
also within the Central Coast.

When she looked closely at the second two, she noticed
something interesting. Point Conception sat at the western point
of that length of coastline that actually angled east-west, so it
might be considered the west-anchor. And Point San Luis sat on a

promontory that gave it a view eastward. *This is kind of a stretch . . . but could be a great theme for my lighthouse piece.*

Now she thought again of the sand dollar—but it had five points, not four. Could she tie it in? Maybe she could, if she included not just the Anglo and Hispanic historical aspects of these lighthouses and their locations, but also the Chumash. She did have some notes about that, and it would be her next file to read.

She would do that soon. For now, she wanted to visit the next lighthouse on her list.

Chapter 12

Chris found her thoughts wandering as she headed north. The eerie quiet of pre-dawn was blessedly free of traffic, even when she merged onto the 101 that would soon be choked with vehicles.

Did this television piece she'd been researching have a shape yet? She liked the themes she'd thought of so far. But she needed a premise, a hook, a title. *Landmarks of California history? Yes, that would play. Warnings? Certainly. Loneliness? Yes. Dedication? Absolutely.*

What would make a person, or an entire family, chose a job that meant isolation, even desolation? Were jobs so scarce in earlier times? Or was being a light keeper not a job, but a calling?

The miles sped by without her taking much notice, as she structured her piece, teasing out the deeper themes and beginning to find the bullet points that she'd use to sell it. But she also knew that with two more visits on her list, she likely had more to learn before all the pieces would fall into place.

She'd read there were once three sister lights, the only so-called Prairie-Victorians that incorporated both home and light tower. Two had burned down—such a tragically frequent occurrence that fuel oil would often be housed in a separate building. The one remaining was today's destination: Point San Luis.

As the cheerful billboards near Pismo Beach slid past, she saw the sun had moved higher in the sky, painting lemon and peach streaks overhead. A lovely segment of the 101 unwound ahead of her and she paid close attention to signs until she saw the turnoff.

The road followed a canyon that sliced through coastal mountains toward Avila Beach until it suddenly opened on a sparkling bay. RVs stood parked end-to-end along the shore, and two piers stretched out into the water. On the mountain side of the coastal road she saw the next lighthouse sign and edged her SUV toward a deserted guard gate.

Moving past it, she noticed one more sign and made a sharp left turn. Now a single-track road began angling slowly upward. *Hope there's no one coming in my direction! I'd have a hell of a time backing all the way down.*

The road had been carved into the steep incline as though following the trail of a snake. She gasped when she emerged from a copse of trees, with nothing in front of her but the unobstructed bay hundreds of feet below. If she weren't careful, she'd sail out over the edge.

Instead, she steadied herself, continuing the serpentine ascent, until she crested at the road's highest point, then began a spiraling descent on the far side of the hill.

As the terrain widened, she saw a collection of wooden buildings perched in a cozy enclave. She parked, noting the sun shone like a beacon from the east. The view of the bay took her breath away. Huge osprey rode thermals overhead; below, white sailboats dotted the bay at their moorings; golden beams sparkled on brilliant blue water; the scooped curvature of the coastline formed a charming haven.

She inhaled, then began walking across the grounds and through the buildings, each of which was a beautifully preserved historic structure, except for a plain-looking utilitarian building farther back from the rim of land.

One printed legend said this lighthouse was also known as the Sentinel of the Sea. What must it have taken the volunteers to shore up the foundations of these historic structures, strengthen the floors and window frames, repaint the walls and trim? Following almost twenty years of neglect, the local Lighthouse Keepers had organized fairly recently, in 1995. And it was worth every hammered nail and brushstroke, for the buildings stood proudly as living monuments to the lives of those who'd come before.

She imagined there'd be a table somewhere with a stamp for this lighthouse. *Might as well add to my collection.* Taking the small notebook from the slender purse slung over her shoulder, she walked through a final display and found what she needed. After inking the rubber stamp, she pressed it into the next blank page of her notebook, admiring the small round graphic that now decorated her page. The surrounding block lettering read POINT SAN LUIS LIGHTHOUSE, CALIFORNIA. In the center was the image of a squat lighthouse with an upper balcony, attached to a house, with the date 1890.

When she exited the building identified as the sound house, the sun had become a brilliant orb hovering closer to the water, casting an amber glow across the landscape and illuminating the windows in theatrical flashes, *Wasn't it morning when I arrived here? I must have lost track of time.*

She stepped into the lighthouse building and began climbing the stairs. It wouldn't take her long to reach the summit this time, as the height of this tower was only 40 feet. When she did, she pressed herself into the tight space surrounding the fourth-order Fresnel, then peered out the high window as sunlight shimmered like copper scales on the water.

Chris had found her brief sojourn at this lighthouse lovely so far, and she knew it'd make a gorgeous location shoot for her cameraman, but she wasn't sure what further information she could gather. Before leaving, she decided to explore the rooms in the residence attached to the tower. She stepped through a connecting door, inhaled the slight must of antiquity, and found beautifully preserved displays of furnishings roped off from the intrusions of the public who must walk through these rooms in droves.

She was about to head back to her car, when she heard a noise—the clank of a dish? Maybe one of the people who worked here would finally make an appearance. Moving toward the sound, she found herself standing in what would have been the family's kitchen. A woman in a costume stacked dishes, removing them from the draining board next to the large sink.

"Oh, hi."

"Hello," the woman said, evidently not surprised to see a visitor.

Not sure what to say, Chris began with, "You certainly have a special place here."

"We like it," the woman said, still not making eye contact.

"I've been giving myself a tour."

"Yes, that's the best way," the woman confirmed. "Cup of tea?"

Surprised at the invitation, Chris stammered, "Uh, yes that'd be nice."

"You can sit over there."

Chris obediently sat in a delicate wooden chair.

"We can see to the east from here, where the dawn breaks."

Well, that was both obvious and enigmatic. I'm not sure what she means, exactly. Still, venturing a reply, Chris offered, "I did notice we can look east from this lighthouse."

A moment later, the woman poured water that she'd apparently already boiled into a large teapot. While the tea steeped, she gathered two cups, two saucers, and a dainty tray with a sugar bowl.

Chris recognized the famous Willow pattern, blue-and-white dishes created by English ceramic artists who'd adapted hand-painted Chinese porcelain pieces. The story depicted was sadly lyrical—a tale of forbidden love—as though she needed any more thoughts on that subject today.

The costumed hostess reached into an old-fashioned ice box, picked up a large glass bottle of milk, decanted some into a small china pitcher, then put the milk jug away. When the tea service items were assembled and delivered, she poured piping hot tea into each cup.

"How do you keep the leaves from coming out with the water?" Chris asked.

The woman looked at her as if she lacked even the most basic elements of education, but then she smiled indulgently "They get trapped inside by the little holes."

"Oh." Chris returned the smile, and the two women sat in companionable silence for several moments.

Chris sipped at her tea, a delicious blend she'd never tasted before. "This is excellent," she commented.

"Yes," said the woman immodestly.

Chris kept silent during another few sips, then resumed their conversation with, "Have you worked here long?"

"Oh, yes," she answered. "Since the beginning. Sometimes it feels like forever."

"Rather lonely I imagine, when no one else is around."

The woman seemed to reflect on this for a while, then her expression turned pensive, her gaze fixed on a distant point only she could see. "New ideas break over the horizon, like the dawn. We each have a purpose," she proclaimed earnestly. "It must be fulfilled. No one can do it for us, only ourselves."

Taken aback by the sudden turn toward philosophy, or spiritual wisdom, or whatever this was, Chris said, "Yes, that's true. Is that what you're doing by working here at the lighthouse?"

"Of course," the woman replied. "Why else would I be here?"

"I . . . I guess that answers it."

"And why you're here, too."

The woman rose and began carrying their dishes to the sink.

"May I help?" Chris asked. "I'm grateful for your hospitality."

Suddenly the woman turned, a beatific smile illuminating her face. "Gratitude opens the way!" she said cheerfully.

A new set of noises made its way inside, female chattering in excited tones, accompanied by multiple footsteps on the wooden stairs. One after another a parade of women—also in costumes—entered the kitchen bearing dishes, platters and baskets in their hands. While continuing a cascade of conversations, they set their offerings as a buffet on the kitchen table, then took turns washing their hands in the sink.

As delicious aromas swirled through the room, Chris watched the activity with a smile, already imagining camera angles and plotting how to negotiate a reenactment to be part of her light-house broadcast.

"Come, dear!" her hostess called, and Chris entered the adjacent dining room, where all the ladies sat expectantly at places set with the lovely antique china, silver, and napkins. "We've set a place for you."

Embarrassed, but also delighted, she took the last chair at the long table and said, 'Thank you."

That seemed to be the cue for conversation to resume, as one by one platters were passed containing a range of dishes honoring local cultures.

"Have some posole," said a Hispanic-looking grandmother. "This was Mission food, Mija."

Mission . . . the original Spanish missions all along the Central Coast.

An Anglo woman handed her a bowl of warm, buttered peas, which must have European origins.

Another platter arrived, this one holding ramekins filled with baked goods. "Gingerbread cake?" she asked.

"No, acorn cake, but the taste is similar," said a guest with long, white braids and ribbons attached to her gown. "From the Chumash people," she explained.

"President Lincoln established our national day of Thanks-giving on November 28, 1863," said the hostess after a hush descended over the table, "just twenty-seven years before our lighthouse was built."

"Since the sinking of the Queen of the Pacific," another guest added.

The hostess lost focus for a moment, her lip quivering.

The white-braided woman filled in. "But our people celebrated the bounty of the harvest for thousands of years before. We thank Spirit for the resources that made this food possible."

The Hispanic and the Anglo women each offered traditional prayers, and then a clattering of silverware against china took over the room and they all ate in silence for a few moments. Chris enjoyed every morsel, unable to determine exactly when she'd last eaten. Then, as suddenly as the gathering had begun, it ended, and the guests gathered plates and platters, washed the china and flatware, then left in a babbling parade.

Chris stood alone at the sink where she dried the last of the plates. She turned to face her hostess and said, "That was wonderful! How very generous of you to include me! I...it was ever so much more than I expected when I came to visit the lighthouse."

"Gratitude opens the way," the woman repeated, that glowing smile overtaking her features again.

That's the second time she's said that. I think she's trying to teach me something.

"Go west next. There is guidance there," her hostess said, pressing something into Chris's hand. After that proclamation, the woman rose, carried her cup to the sink, and left the room. Chris imagined she'd be back in a moment, but after several minutes when she didn't return, Chris could only assume their visit had ended. Gathering her small purse from the back of the chair where she'd hung it, Chris rose, left the building and went to her car.

The grounds had now been plunged into darkness with only a rim of deep Prussian blue painted across the horizon. Far below, the bay was devoid of color, its outline etched in coastal lights that glittered like a necklace of tiny diamonds curving on black velvet.

She opened her car door and then, sitting in her driver's seat, she took out her notebook and jotted down some of the conversation she'd had with the woman, imagining it would make interesting, if somewhat enigmatic dialogue for her television documentary.

But the exchange with yet another mysterious lighthouse woman, the long drive, and the strange circumstances had left her exhausted. *Maybe just a quick nap before driving the rest of the way home.* She reclined her seat and closed her eyes.

The first light crept quietly over the hillside, her lighthouse hostess's words filtered into her sleep: "New ideas break over the horizon, like the dawn."

Chapter 13

Del had become an expert at research over the years. Certainly old-fashioned legwork was the foundation of all good detecting and he relied on it.

Though he continued to hone his expertise using the latest internet search tools, he still found library archives, newspaper article "morgue" files, and repositories of vital records to be the most reliable and comprehensive resources. After all, an internet search could only reveal what someone had scanned and uploaded. Plenty of material had never been digitally archived.

If he'd thought about journalists at any earlier point in his life, he supposed he'd have thought of their work mostly as interviews and angles: interview their subject, then figure out an angle for their article. At crime scenes, he'd mostly thought of them as pests.

But Chris Christian was every bit as much a researcher as he was. He'd surmised as much from a quick look at the file folders in her home office. And during their conversation, she'd confirmed the specific threads she'd been following.

A chill ran across Del's scalp and down his back. *I'm still acting as if I had a real conversation with her. But it was a dream!*

It'd been something of a relief to spend a few days absorbed with his actual job. Captain Sandoval had assigned him two more cases for the Special Projects Unit, and these had required driving both north and south for meetings and interviews.

As usual, tonight he'd grabbed a stack of work when he'd left his office. With tomorrow his day off, he knew he'd probably be spending part of it catching up on the ever-present paperwork that plagued every law enforcement officer he'd ever met.

His dinner of microwaved lasagna had sufficed to take the edge off his hunger and he bit into a dessert of an apple with a slice of cheddar, papers spread out on his dining table in place of dishes that now rested in the kitchen sink.

But he'd also brought home his Chris Christian file and he reached first for the small notebook. Chris's handwriting had become somewhat familiar, as were the two lighthouse stamps she'd printed on two previous dates. He flipped further through the sheafs, but stopped when he saw a stamp from a third lighthouse.

I swear this wasn't here before. Have I been that careless? He looked at it closely. In the inked image, a rather short lighthouse seemed to be attached to a house, and around it block letters read "Point San Luis Lighthouse, California." Next to it, a second stamp indicated a date from last November, so once again he had an indication of when she'd been there.

Now, to overcome any possibility the little book held more stamps he'd overlooked, he turned through each page carefully. Though there were blank pages randomly spaced, there were indeed only the three lighthouse stamps.

Yet I feel certain this third one wasn't here last time I looked. He put the book down and his eyes lost focus. The papers on his table seemed to be swimming across his field of vision. *I have absolutely no explanation for that . . . none that I can stand to think about right now.*

Del pushed his chair back and headed for the recliner in his living room, sinking down into it, exhausted. What he really needed was to clear his head. Perhaps that would be a better use of his time tomorrow, rather than trying to plow through more paperwork.

Closing his eyes, he began to make a plan for his well-deserved day off. His tried-and-true techniques were running and hiking. In Los Angeles, running had long been his method of choice, and he'd availed himself of many public trails from Griffith Park to the Hollywood Reservoir. Great as those were, the Central Coast offered a beautiful range of options.

Though there were several a bit farther inland near SLO, he favored those closer to the coast. The Reservoir Canyon Loop Trail near Morro Bay was a good moderate choice, as was the Bluff Trail in Montana de Oro State Park near Los Osos. The Santa Rosa Creek Trail was a sweet one, running quietly alongside the partially wooded neighborhoods of Cambria. But what appealed to him was the idea of taking a run along the ocean. The Bluff Trail would be just the ticket.

With that settled, Del reached for some music to steady his nerves. Nothing grounded him better than blues. He reached for his contemporary Keb Mo, a favorite recording artist whose album "Just Like You" had won the musician a Grammy a couple of year earlier. Still a fan of vinyl, Del dropped the needle on "Perpetual Blues Machine" and sat back, tapping his foot at the walkin' blues guitar rhythm, the sultry harmonica, and that soulful voice that held strains from its Louisiana and Texas roots.

"Now you've gone, and I'm glad," the singer mourned. "That we didn't let it go too bad." Del had been known to play tunes as background while doing chores—sanding a table smooth, or cleaning his kitchen, singing along as though he had company. But now, soothing though the music was, Del suddenly felt the lyric too close to the unaccountable loss he felt about Chris, so he rose to choose another album.

Jimmy Bartow was a long time favorite. Del had actually met the older man years earlier, as his uncle had befriended Jim following a local concert, back when his Aunt Em and her husband had lived in New York. Bartow's concert had been held at The Harlem School of the Arts, where he also taught. His impressive teaching credentials, which included Hunter and Vassar Colleges, hinted at his passion for curating historical blues.

But he also wrote original songs in the traditional blues tradition, and recorded several albums, starting with "Blues Enough."

Del dropped the needle on the title tune and sat back to listen. The guitar came to life first establishing a cadence with bass tones, while fingers shifting chords rasped along the strings in a melodic repetition. Then the singer became a presence in the room, the warmth in his voice an aural kindling of a soulful flame.

> Leave me alone, I got troubles of my own
> Leave me alone, I got troubles of my own
> I got blues enough for the both of us.

Despite the lyrics, which demanded the listener keep his distance, the loneliness in Bartow's voice issued an invitation to lessen the burden. How could someone not even here physically feel so close? It worked with music. And evidently, it also worked with dreams. If he could sense Chris's proximity while awake, would he welcome it? The answer seemed, at least for now, to be beyond Del's reach. Drifting off to sleep in his chair, Del listened as, right on cue, the singer continued:

> I feel for you baby, but I can't reach it
> I feel for you baby, but I can't reach it
> The grass ain't no greener, but the roots may grow deeper.

Del had wakened sometime during the night and made his way to bed. He awoke refreshed and took his planned outing. For the rest of the day, he'd catch up on domestic chores: laundry, cleaning, food shopping, and a few other personal errands.

The run along the escarpment high above the waves proved the perfect place to let ocean wind blow out the fog of worry and restore enough clarity to frame the right questions, if not yet the answers he needed.

What do I need to do next about Chris Christian? He would hit the library stacks again on Monday, when he could access the larger collection in SLO. That felt solid and reasonable.

If research was first on his go-to list for problem-solving, then going to a mentor was second. There were, of course, the "bejeweled" family women: his grandmother Sapphire, his Aunt Emerald, his mother Ruby, and his sister Tanzanite, nicknamed Tanzi, or sometimes "Semi-Precious."

Talking with Granny Sparkle was no longer an option. Neither could he ask his late mother. It might make sense to call his Aunt Em, though they'd never discussed the Gift, of which the family rumor mill reported she'd been jealous. He did love her, though, and always felt close to her husband Isaiah.

Meanwhile, his conversation with Tanzi had given him a clue or two. And her words had taken his anxiety down a notch by helping him to accept that he might, indeed, have inherited a version of this ancestral gift, something those before him had utilized and survived intact.

The only other person he could think of who qualified as a mentor was Kuyama. She truly was an elder—not of his own, but of the local Chumash tribe. *Don't know why she popped into my head, but I trust the instinct.*

Kuyama Freeland had begun her career years earlier as an activist, later became an author, and meanwhile served by turns as spokeswoman, educator, speaker, and member of the Tribal Council. He'd enjoyed speaking with her several weeks earlier, and had been invited to contact her any time he wished. He would call in the morning to see whether he might meet with her.

Chapter 14

Chris sensed the gentle pressure of early daylight on her eyelids. As they fluttered open, she was surprised to find herself resting in her living room recliner.

While she tried to process the memory of the previous evening, something slipped from her hand and onto the floor. Looking down, she saw it was a sand dollar.

What the—? Why would I be holding a sea shell?

Then she remembered—she'd been jotting down notes about her lighthouse visits, looking for themes for her article. *Right! And I went to Point San Luis. Must have found it there. And it's a reminder that I wanted to look up the Chumash symbol.*

She stood, walked into her master suite. Refreshed enough to know she'd slept well, even if it hadn't been in her bed, she also felt more settled than she had in quite a while, glad to be home, and even gladder to be on the trail of an article that engaged her.

While she showered, the events of the San Luis light came back to her: the property with its gorgeous view, the short light tower, deserted while she looked around.

Until she met that strange woman in the kitchen. *Strange, maybe, but kind.* She had offered her tea, then invited her to join that group of women for their historic reenactment meal.

They'd all seemed so serious, so eager to share with her. Did they feel they had to justify their celebration, explain their presence? Well, they had just as much right to be there as she did, and evidently they'd made extensive preparations for their gathering.

They'd been so colorful, if eccentric—they'd certainly add color to this piece she wanted to do. But could she contact them to reappear for her video shoot? Somehow, she doubted it. Their gathering had seemed ritualized and private, not frivolous, and not social in the traditional sense. If it had been a fund raiser, no one had made mention of their cause. So the historically decorated rooms themselves would have to suffice for her shoot, and she would do enough research to bring in relevant historical facts.

Chris dried her hair and pulled on her favorite sweats and socks. Today felt like a Sunday. Was it? She'd lost track, but it felt delicious to work from home, outline her piece, read through her files, get her ducks in a row before her next outing. *Maybe I'll whip up an omelet.*

In the kitchen, she grated some cheddar from the block she found in her fridge. She heated butter in her favorite skillet, spun a couple of eggs with a fork and tossed in some dill and basil from her spice rack. After making another pot of coffee and buttering some hot toast, she carried her breakfast back to her desk.

Jotting down notes between bites, by the time she'd finished eating, her writer-juices were flowing. She pushed away her plate, rolled up her sleeves, powered up her notebook computer, and began typing the outline. "California History Illuminated by Lighthouses," she began. Today would be a satisfyingly productive day.

Chris had written more by mid-afternoon than she expected. Not only was her outline complete, she'd also finished her on-camera script for the first three of the four segments she'd planned.

Daylight seemed to be dimming, but she paid little attention. Her writing finished for now, she picked up her research, starting with the sand dollar. In Chumash symbology, it signified something about the sun, though she couldn't quite grasp the concept. "The sun rises from the east and goes to the west, and all the spirits follow him. They leave their bodies."

That reminds of something I read. But what? Oh, yes! The skeletons of the sand dollars. What they leave behind when they die. What the Chumash believe is more poetic . . . a spiritual interpretation of the science.

Next she read about Point Conception, which would be her fourth lighthouse destination. She knew that, while the Coast Guard still controlled the lighthouse itself, the surrounding property was owned by a private ranch, or maybe two, and she'd heard access was difficult, or maybe even impossible. Still, she'd had success at the others, finding them open and mostly deserted.

She began reviewing her files, which contained more material than she'd remembered collecting. *Maybe I won't have to spend time in the library before my visit after all.*

First, Chris found, reprinted by the U.S. Lighthouse Society, a personal account by Harry Weeks called "The Keeper's Log," an account from his boyhood that had been edited by his wife Alice Weeks, which provided enough history to add color to her video.

Second, she knew that at this point the Fresnel was still in place, though previous research had revealed that these elaborate and heavy instruments were more and more frequently being removed, both for safety and for preservation.

Next, she came across an article about a Chumash elder and activist named Kuyama Freeland, who'd participated in protests at several sites in the Central Coast, either to protect native heritage or the environment—or both.

Freeland referred to her friend and fellow elder Pilulaw Khus, who'd famously brought a lawsuit in 1993 against a developer determined to plough down a small hill to make visible the Walmart he planned to build near Highway 101. The lawsuit required archeological reports, all of which confirmed 5,000 year-old remains of a village and of its dead, making it a sacred site. Ultimately the developer had to withdraw.

But Kuyama also pointed out that Native grave sites had been destroyed at other locations throughout the region to make way for modern installations: missile silos at Vandenberg Air Force Base, a housing subdivision in Pismo, the nuclear power plant at Diablo Canyon, and many more.

Chris wondered whether she could contact Ms. Freeland, to interview her in person, not so much about grave sites, but about the Chumash history of the Point Conception area. The article mentioned a location where the elder could receive mail, and Chris made a note of it. Perhaps she could stop by there tomorrow en route to the lighthouse.

Having come across the mention of Vandenberg Airforce Base, Chris hunted up her Space files. Though she hadn't added much to them recently, she had a long-standing connection to NASA and an abiding interest in space.

Years earlier, she'd been the youngest reporter for the Apollo Soyuz Mission, and had cut her teeth as the junior member of the Consolidated Press team in both Canaveral and Houston.

She riffled through the NASA: Apollo-Soyuz file, finding pages of official NASA briefs, C.P. telex printouts, and even photos of herself with the experienced journalists who'd become her mentors. She'd stayed in touch with Reed Moore and with Bob Mitchell, relying on them through the years for guidance. Sometimes she'd needed to whine; other times she'd just needed to bounce ideas.

The NASA PR office had always been available to provide information to the press, and she'd maintained trusted sources at the agency. But the military operated under a completely different mandate. Vandenberg was a tightly controlled area and she'd never been invited to a launch—though she'd been out to Edwards AFB for Shuttle landings. With Vandenberg's proximity to Point Conception, how did its presence impact the region? She had no idea, and wondered whether it'd be relevant to her reporting. In any case, she had no detailed file to peruse here at home.

But in her "Point Conception" file, a separate news piece said that the area was nostalgically known as "the last perfect place" in California. She could easily imagine why locals from Santa Barbara, Gaviota, and Lompoc gave it such a romantic name: rolling hills and carved escarpments tumbling to the sea, secluded white sandy beaches, blustery fresh air and a feeling that no one else on Earth could intrude.

Would developers change all that? One day would the pristine landscape be peppered with condos and sliced up into gated communities? Or would some magnanimous bene-volence inspire a donor to bequeath the land to some kind of conservancy? One could only hope for such an outcome.

Meanwhile, she'd do her best to enjoy the last, perfect place while she could.

Delmar's day progressed in a pleasingly logical order. By making several phone calls from home in the morning, he was able to arrange his meetings in a sequence both chronological and geographic.

Kuyama Freeland had agreed to meet with him at 1 p.m., so Del planned a stop for brunch at Country Touch Café on El Camino Real, not far from where she lived in Atascadero, up and over highway 46.

The café had been established in 1985, and by now was a neighborhood icon. He enjoyed their signature omelette—filled with smoky bacon, mushrooms, grilled onion, avocado, tomato, melted jack cheese and topped with sour cream—a piping-hot plate of comfort food if ever there was one.

The meal was so satisfying, it helped take the edge off the nerves he could feel beginning to jangle again at the thought of the questions he wanted to ask the elder. He would ease into the subject, he thought, rather than blurting out his pre-posterous sounding claim of having detailed conversations with a spirit. Perhaps understanding more about the history of her people with its own spirituality would give him context and reassurance.

Del arrived promptly at the appointed hour and found his hostess's door standing ajar, and her voice reached him from within.

"Come in," she said.

As he stepped inside, he saw her tall figure illuminated by light from the west-facing window to her left. Her long white hair seemed to glisten like an illuminated aura around her head and shoulders, her presence commanding yet gentle.

Beside her stood an attentive dog of mixed breed, who didn't bark, but looked directly into Del's eyes as though inquiring as to his errand.

"So nice to see you again, Deputy," Kuyama said. "Let's sit together in the kitchen."

She led the way, her dog at her heels, and he followed. Her cottage was larger on the inside than it'd seemed on the outside, cozy and inviting, yet airy and bright. A lovely oceanscape hung on her kitchen wall, and he thought it might be a Miranda Jones painting.

"Please make that Delmar," he invited.

"And this is Atishwin." Kuyama nodded at her dog, whose eyes came up to meet Del's.

"Thank you—both of you—for making the time."

"Of course. I always have time for those who serve."

They sat together at a small table, and he noticed she'd set out handmade pottery—three cups and a teapot, a fragrant blend already brewing.

"Expecting someone else?" he asked.

She held his gaze for a moment, her light gray eyes mesmerizing. "Perhaps," she said, offering no further explanation. "How may I help?"

Delmar let out a long breath, then surprised himself by blurting out, "I think I may be receiving visitations."

Kuyama lifted the teapot and poured something aromatic into two of the cups. "These are unexpected?" she asked.

"Well, I may have invited them."

"That is usually the case," she confirmed, nodding. "And this is part of your work?"

Del held the thick cup and let it warm his hands, which had suddenly gone cold. *She doesn't seem surprised by anything I'm saying. I suppose that makes this easier.* "A woman—a journalist—is missing. She's been gone for a while, but since she travels extensively for her reporting, no one really noticed. Until they did."

"Yes. I believe I've heard something about her."

"You've probably seen her on television. Her special reports are excellent, extensively researched. And she tells a story to draw in her audience, that's for sure."

"And she has drawn you."

Del nodded, then took a sip. He didn't usually like tea, but remarked, "This is excellent. A bit smoky."

"Lapsang Souchong. Most coffee drinkers do like the flavor."

How would she know I drink coffee? Probably the same way she knows a lot of things.

"You're investigating her disappearance?" Kuyama inquired.

"Unofficially, yes. So I can't give it my full attention. There's no doubt in my mind that she is—or was—on an assignment. It's what she does—or did. If she was onto something—a lead, a thread, a clue—she'd pursue it. And if it put her in danger, then it's my job to figure out what she was following. But this has become somehow . . . personal, too," he admitted.

Kuyama stirred her tea for a moment, then said. "I believe there may be two issues here. One is the story she was researching, which is tied to her work, and to yours."

"Right," Del agreed.

"The other is your . . ." Kuyama seemed to search for the right word. "Your attunement to her. Or perhaps, your receptivity."

Del could feel his skin prickle, and could only imagine what she might see as she stared into his eyes. "I . . . You're right. There may be. . ." Now it was his turn to compose his thoughts and reach for words. "My grandmother had what she called The Gift. Some call it Second Sight, or The Guidance. But it was more than that. She was able to see and hear those who had passed on."

Kuyama stopped stirring her tea and put down her spoon. "Your grandmother spoke with you about this?"

"She did. I was young. Too young to ask more about it. And then later, well, my training, my work as an investigator . . . there's very little room for hunches or intuitions, at least officially."

"That surprises me," she commented. "I would think intuition would be an important tool for an investigator."

"You're correct," he confirmed. "And it's acknowledged anecdotally. But we have to prepare cases based on tangibles, nail down details with first-hand accounts, back these up with physical evidence. They have to stand up in court, or the work is for naught."

"Yes, I see. But Truth uncovers what is true, however we arrive at its proof."

Del let that insight sink in.

"Do other members of your family also have your grandmother's gift?" she asked.

"No. Well—anecdotally—I do. Or so Granny said. My sister —she's the only one I've talked to about it—she confirmed what Granny Sparkle believed."

"But you've never experienced it yourself before now?"

Del inhaled. "No. Or if I had hints, I dismissed them. Tried to prove it was the old wive's tale most people think it is. I guess I've been running from it, or trying to. But maybe . . . it might be the reason I became an investigator. Sometimes a case just opens up in a way that doesn't make sense, until it suddenly clicks into place."

Kuyama sat quietly, then said, "Some talents only appear when we're mature enough to manage them."

"That's another thing Granny said!" Del confirmed. "My sister reminded me. Granny Blue said this would likely show up when I was older."

Kuyama smiled. "I think perhaps we've put together the pieces of one corner of your puzzle."

Del pressed his lips together. "I suppose we have. The 'acceptance' corner. I've got to accept that I have some version of the Gift that Granny had. But does it have to be so . . . I mean, I had a full conversation with this woman!"

Kuyama's eyes widened. "You saw and heard her?"

Del looked down into his empty tea cup. "Either I sat across the table from her and we compared notes on cases. Or I dreamed I did."

The dog walked to his mistress and looked up. Kuyama reached her hand down to touch her pet's head, nodding as she did. "So this is how those who need to reach you can do so—in dreams."

"Yes. But Tanzi, my sister, says Granny spoke to them in plain daylight and wide awake."

"I believe it is different for each of us."

Del looked up sharply into Kuyama's face. "You said us."

Kuyama returned his gaze, but did not elaborate. "Is there something more you need from this woman?"

"I'm not sure. Well, yes. If there was foul play, if she was. . . she might not remember, but she knows more than she's told me so far."

"And she, like you, has a sense of purpose."

He leaned in. "Explain."

"Work projects may begin dispassionately, but they can ignite us, possess us, until we reach completion. I know this from my own work."

Del nodded.

"But if that work is interrupted, we may feel compelled to finish what we've started. We may feel no one else can fulfill this mission. And we may be quite correct in this feeling."

Del considered her insight, feeling the truth of it as his thoughts wandered to the projects on his own work bench: the cases that fascinated, that clamored for his attention, that wouldn't let him alone day or night—including this one.

"Let's talk for a moment about work, about how it becomes a calling. Do you mind?" she asked.

"Mind? Please, continue."

"There was a time I became very involved with a particular issue. Some land that is sacred to my people came under threat. We felt we were called to protect it, so we staged an occupation.

This required quite a bit of inconvenience and discomfort. But we ignored that. The issue was too important to us. The land was near Point Conception. In fact, I'd like to show you something. I'll be right back."

Kuyama left the kitchen and Del watched as her dog followed, its nails clicking on the linoleum floor. *God, I'm tired. What's wrong with me? I'll have to stop for a coffee-to-go before I drive back.*

Del pushed his cup away and put his head down on his folded arms. *I'll just rest my eyes while she looks for whatever she wants to show me.*

Chapter 15

Kuyama returned to the kitchen with a file folder, and was not surprised to find that Deputy Delmar was resting with his head down on her kitchen table.

Neither was she surprised when her dog began to whine and tilt its head to one side, sensing their second guest had arrived. Kuyama walked to her front door where a blond woman stood.

"This is very nice of you," the woman said, "And on such short notice. I'm Christine."

"Yes, I've been expecting you," Kuyama said. "Please come this way." Fascinated to see what would happen next, she gestured toward the empty chair on the far side of the table. "I'll make more tea," she added, pouring water into her kettle, which she placed on the stove. When she turned around, Del was awake—or seemed to be. *Is this one of his waking dreams? It must be, because they are seeing one another and communicating.*

"You're here!" Chris said to Del. "I thought that might be your vehicle out front. I wasn't sure when I'd see you again, but this is perfect. I've gathered some files for you. They're in my bag."

"Good," he said. "And I see you know Kuyama."

"Well, we've just met, but she was kind enough to invite me over. I'm going to visit Point Conception, and I wanted to ask her about it."

Kuyama stood observing her guests. *This is most unusual. Apparently I can hear their conversation. But can they hear, or see me? Yes, Christine sees me. Does Delmar?*

"Interesting," he said. "You've been visiting lighthouses. So this is the next one on your list?"

"Exactly," Chris confirmed. "It'll be my next broadcast piece. I visit the locations, line up the interviews, before I get confirmation from the station or schedule the shoot with my crew."

"Hmm, I figured you worked on assignment. Didn't realize you found your own."

Kuyama found that interesting, too. *This means she has autonomy, and wouldn't have to be in touch with colleagues. She seems to have no idea she would no longer be able to meet with them. But she is reaching out . . . to those whom she can reach.*

"These days I mostly choose my own," Chris replied. "The lighthouses are fascinating. Each has its own significance. But I think this next one might be the most complex of all, not just the lighthouse, but the surrounding land. Lots of conflicting interests." Chris turned toward Kuyama. "And you have a key part of the story."

Now Del looked toward Kuyama as well, making eye contact just the way he had during their "waking" conversation. "Really?"

Kuyama looked from one to the other of her guests, wanting to add a comment. *But do I dare? Will I disrupt the communication? Well . . . nothing ventured. . . .*

"Just before you arrived, Christine, I mentioned to Delmar that, some time back, I became very involved with a particular issue. It had to do with the land near Point Conception, which is sacred to my people."

Seeing she had the rapt attention of both her guests, Kuyama poured more hot water into the tea pot, then let it steep as she began to explain.

"We call the area Humqaq, and it lies at the center of a bitter controversy."

"Is this about money? About development?" Del asked. "Oh, the occupation was about oil, wasn't it?"

"Hmm, I think it might be about the military," Chris countered.

"You're both right, in that my people often find themselves in battles over land use," Kuyama said, pouring tea into each of the three cups. "Delmar, you are correct. In 1979 my friend Pilulaw Khus, an elder of the Northern Chumash Bear Clan, was one of our leaders of a nearly year-long occupation to resist construction of a natural gas refinery. We won that battle. You see, we Chumash are the Keepers of the Gate, so we had no choice but protect it.

"But Christine has pinpointed the situation that will develop next," Kuyama continued. *She may already be seeing into the future, either as part of her natural ability, or part of her transition . . . or both.* "A clash of our spiritual traditions with one of the most exalted technological projects of the government."

"Vandenberg," Del said. "The space race."

"The U.S. military consider the area around Point Conception to be of strategic importance," Kuyama said.

"It's the placement I think," Chris added. "From what I've read, they consider it a 'remote' location. But more importantly, it's a key location for launching into polar orbit without flying over populated areas."

"You're well informed," Del commented.

"I've done some writing about space," Chris offered.

"But," Kuyama interjected, "the region is also strategic for the Chumash—spiritually strategic."

"I'm not sure I understand," Chris said, putting a hand around her warm tea cup. "You mentioned the Gate."

Though it might cause her great anxiety, I must answer her question. "In our culture, it is the location where the souls of the dead depart for Shimilaqsha, Chumash realm of the dead."

The three sat in silence for a long moment. Even Atishwin sat perfectly still.

"Humqaq," Chris said quietly.

"It means 'the raven comes,'" Kuyama explained. "It's also known as the Western Gate, the place the souls of the dead leave the Earth and begin the long journey to heaven."

Kuyama worried her pronouncement would trigger a reaction in Christine, perhaps an overwhelming one, and the elder had no wish to manipulate anyone's journey, especially one so thoughtful and measured. But the woman's spirit still took little notice of its changed circumstances. *She must process her transition in her own way, in her own time.*

"What an irony," Chris remarked.

"Because it's a departure point in both cultures?" Del said.

"A departure point for the heavens," Chris confirmed.

"In both realities, souls are aiming at the stars," Kuyama agreed. "Our traditions are considered myths. Actually, I embrace the term. The Chumash are the star-gazers, myth-makers, navigators."

Kuyama felt she was on the edge of saying too much to non tribal members. Yet nothing could have prepared her for this: an investigator who could see and hear beyond the veil, and a visitant not yet aware of her own transitional circumstance. They were here for her guidance, and would not have come, had they not needed it.

"Siliyuk is the Whole World in Chumash mythology. This word also signifies governing body. The Mission system brought by the Spanish attempted to strip these spiritual guides of their legitimacy, but they could not deprive them of their power. Despite many converts to Christianity, the traditional ritual practices continued in secrecy.

"There were important ceremonies keyed to the sun, stars and planets, and in tune with the solstices. A historian from the early 1900s interviewed Fernando Librado Kitsepawit, who was born and raised at Mission San Buenaventura, but whose parents were from Santa Cruz Island. Librado knew the ancient languages and customs. He told the historian that if a man observed the virtues that belonged to the rays of the sun, he would be like a ray in the world. He would have noble feelings to help his neighbors."

"Simple and poetic," Chris observed. "So I imagine there was a ceremony connected to the Western Gate. Did they . . . do you—" Chris paused, then asked, "If it's a point of departure, then is the belief that those who die go on to a farther destination, that their paths continue?"

Kuyama inhaled. *This is a critical question. I must answer well.* "Yes. Just because we move into spirit doesn't mean we are no longer ourselves." She paused as Chris seemed to take this in with equanimity. "There's a tale about a group of old men who assembled to speak with a wise man. They asked, 'And those who die, how do they come to be born again?' The wise man answered, "They follow the sun.""

"Toward the west," Del said.

"The Western Gate," Chris echoed. "The symbol of the sand dollar."

Kuyama looked at her guests, wondering now whether she herself were in a dream, the situation was so unusual. *But this is not about me. This is a soul trying to find her way, and she has successfully reached two of us who can help her. I am sure that's why she's here. She's even accepting the significance of the Western Gate. If only I can guide her carefully. . . .*

Del remarked, "You were on a couple of other stories we talked about: Wilhelm Chernak, the Clarke house. So why lighthouses all of a sudden?"

Kuyama saw that Chris began to tremble. *No! If a tide of memories rises too high, she'd be swallowed up and swept away!* "Perhaps," she chimed in, "they're lighting your way."

Chris turned to look at her, gratitude and relief in her expression. "You're right, they are," she agreed. "I found a Charles Dickens quotation." Chris reached into her bag, drew out her ever-present notebook and flipped it open. "'There are dark shadows on the earth, but its lights are stronger in the contrast,' he wrote."

"Yes," Kuyama confirmed.

"Makes sense," Del said.

"I had sort of lost my bearings," Chris added, "until I started visiting the lighthouses. Now that I've begun this new piece about them, about California history, I've got . . . I've got a new assignment."

"And something more," Kuyama added.

"Right. They're navigation points. Everything else is floating, while they stay put."

"Like a ship finding its way along the shore," Del observed.

The dog sat up and whined.

Kuyama's hand touched his head. "I know, Atishwin. She's ready to leave now."

Delmar sat bolt upright, awakened by the dog's whining.

"Sorry!" he exclaimed. "I didn't mean to be rude. Must've been more tired than I thought. I—" His gaze fell on the third teacup and Kuyama's hand touched his forearm.

"It's all right," she said, evidently trying to calm him.

"Was someone . . . you had another guest? You should have wakened me and kicked me out." He made to stand up, but her hand pressed his arm.

"Just breathe for a moment," she suggested.

"I think. . . ." He could feel his heart start to hammer in his chest. "I had another one of those dreams."

"It was more than a dream, Delmar. I saw her too."

"Jesus!"

Kuyama laughed lightly. 'Well, perhaps for some people."

"No, I didn't mean—" Del's gaze strafed the kitchen, looking for evidence. "She was here?!"

"It's startling, I know. But let's think it through, see if our memories of the visit are aligned."

Del nodded, willing himself to regain his composure, use logic to bring himself back into focus. As he did, the entire conversation came back to him as though it'd happened just moments earlier. *Which it did!* He had to settle himself with another deep inhalation.

"She came to see you, as I did."

"Yes, and for much the same reason," Kuyama agreed.

"Seeking guidance."

"Yes, she is an earnest seeker after Truth," she said. "For her, it comes in themes and metaphors, as it does to all writers. This is what she knows, how she understands the world."

"If she's . . . if her body has died, doesn't she have to let go at some point?" Del asked, the question filling him with pain.

"At her own point," Kuyama said calmly.

Delmar nodded, stood, and made his way toward her front door. Pausing, he turned to her and said, "Thank you again. Thanks hardly seems adequate."

"Each of us serves in our own way. And you filled in more of your puzzle pieces." Kuyama smiled, her eyes taking on a sparkle that reminded him of his granny.

Del looked down at her dog, who was gazing up at him earnestly. "Remind me, what's your dog's name again?"

"Atishwin," she said. "It means Spirit Helper."

Delmar sat behind the wheel for a moment to get his bearings, both literally and figuratively. At this location in Atascadero, he was close enough to northern SLO County Sheriff's headquarters to stop by for a visit with the weekend crew. But he was in no mood for a casual session of chewing the fat with his fellow officers. He needed to reflect, think, and reconnoiter, all of which was best done at home.

As he drove, the scene at Kuyama's kitchen table replayed itself. *Make that scenes, plural,* he thought, realizing he'd had back-to-back conversations in normal and then in altered states of mind.

It was now obvious that Kuyama, like him, and like his grandmother before him, had this Gift, whatever it was. She could hear and see "spirits in transition" as she referred to them. Her calm awareness meant she'd long ago accepted the Gift for herself. And she'd certainly had a calming effect on him, just as he'd hoped.

But she'd also been some sort of enabler, or conduit. Otherwise, why would Christine have come to her place? And how did Kuyama seem to know in advance that she would?

Del couldn't answer of these questions. Indeed, they all led to the overriding one that repeated itself in his brain: Why me? he kept asking himself. He could understand, now, why Kuyama had been willing to help him. She'd made this same journey herself at some earlier point in her life. But why did Chris Christian keep popping into his dreams?

Is it because I'm the only one actually investigating her disappearance? Can the answer be that simple?

Intellectually, he knew that was, indeed, the simplest answer. But he also knew there was more to it. Delmar couldn't deny his connection to Chris, any more than he could refuse to admit the synchronicity of visiting Kuyama at the same time that she did.

Back when she was just a "case," he'd been able to keep her at a safe distance by viewing her on video. On the other hand, he now admitted, he'd also been able to indulge his own fantasies by imagining what it would be like to know her. He'd been drawn to her. How? First, emotionally. Partly, this was because of her story-telling skills. Watching that adoption piece of hers had pulled at his heartstrings, even though knew he was being expertly manipulated by an experienced reporter.

Second, he was drawn to her intellectually for her ability to string clues together and leap across the synapses of missing information to create plausible theories. This was a skill they shared and it made them colleagues—or could, if they truly had the chance to work together.

Third, there was something more. Before these dream-visitations, he'd have put it down to physical attraction. She was beautiful, sexy in an understated way, graceful. But these dream-sessions had rattled him to such a degree he'd felt any potential heat turn stone cold. Or so he'd thought.

Today, he'd felt . . . warmth again. *Was it compassion? Sympathy? Even grief?* He could draw no conclusion, as he knew nothing more about her fate. What he did know was that she'd be heading to Point Conception. And he was prepared to bet a new stamp would show up on what was now a blank page of her notebook.

Chapter 16

Chris had packed her briefcase, including her laptop, and a small duffle before leaving her condo, so when she left Kuyama's home, she headed south on the 101 and bypassed the exit for her place in Santa Maria.

Unlike her other lighthouse destinations, this one would be inaccessible by car, so she headed toward the town of Lompoc. Then she'd make her way to Jalama Beach and from there, she planned to hike to Point Conception.

The trail would have its challenges. The distance would be about nine miles round trip, but if she climbed upward to get a higher vantage point on the lighthouse, it could be a bit longer. Tomorrow would be winter solstice—the year's shortest day—so she planned to leave early. She'd also consulted a local chart and planned her sojourn to the lighthouse property during the lowest tide. The point would be windy and negotiating over rocks and rough terrain would be enough to deal with, without trying to avoid crashing waves or rising water.

Her excursion would need most of a day, and she wanted to start fresh and give herself time to prepare, so the adventure was set for tomorrow. The state park at Jalama had three tiny cabins to rent, and she'd left a reservation on their voice mail. The system worked as did many camp sites: leave payment in a provided envelope, then deposit it into a lock box. The cabin would give her a staging area, a shelter if the weather turned, and a place to rest after her long hike. She didn't want to drive home, and she preferred not to sleep in her car again. And this evening, she could review her notes, process her meeting with Kuyama and Delmar, and get a good night's sleep right at the trailhead.

She was barely past Santa Maria when she turned off the 101 at exit 166, surprised to realize the proximity of her home to the coastal region that now held her interest. She stayed on East Union Valley Parkway, or the 135, for a short segment, but then forked westward onto Highway 1 as it headed for the coast.

As she followed the lovely, rural route, afternoon sun alternately streamed through the windshield, then momentarily hid behind a hill or a tree, teasing with golden light. As she drove, she mentally reviewed the gear in her duffle: sturdy hiking shoes, a small backpack and a flashlight she could attach to one of its front straps. She'd carry a bottle of water and a light, waterproof jacket, as the weather at the point could turn misty enough to make her feel clammy. She always kept an extra fleece, and a sleeping bag in the back of her SUV, as well as a few other emergency provisions, given that she lived in an earthquake zone.

Highway 1 angled past Vandenberg, then carved and curved its way through mountain canyons becoming more and more of a rural road past private ranches and undeveloped properties until it delivered her to the eastern edge of Lompoc.

Since she had no real business there, and no time for sightseeing, Chris continued past. According to her map, she would travel twenty miles south from here to arrive at a spot situated between Point Arguello and Point Conception.

She turned off the main road when she reached Jalama Road, then wound through the coastal hills until an expansive glimpse of Pacific stretched across her view and railroad tracks ran parallel to the coast across her path. The road took a hard left, then looped over the tracks at Cojo Bay Road to take her north again until she reached Jalama County Beach Park.

Chris spotted the cabins atop an escarpment overlooking the beach, and pulled her vehicle into the parking lot. She stepped out of her SUV and inhaled the fresh breeze, an anodyne to her recent tensions. For a moment she closed her eyes against the bright sun just beginning to descend toward the Pacific.

I should figure out which tiny house is mine. Names were hand-lettered on cards slid into glassed-in boxes on the fronts of two of the cabins, yet all three appeared unoccupied. The key to the third hung next to the empty glass box, so she assumed there must be a time lag between reservations taken and the manager's marking the cabins. Budget cuts made this kind of lag all too common.

She opened the front door and walked directly across the one small room to the sliding door that led to a small balcony overlooking the spectacular view. *Perfect*, she thought. *Maybe I'll stay the week instead of just two nights!*

She'd heard there were similar cabins at Lake Cachuma, and she could understand the peaceful appeal of a lake. And yet for her, it was the ocean than cleansed and challenged. The inland lake would almost always have warmer weather, with the cool water offering respite. The ocean location would generally be cooler and even cold at night, and would sometimes be shrouded in fog. Yet the temperamental nature of the coast suited her better than the steady certitude of sunshine.

A few minutes later, she'd brought her necessaries inside. But before she settled in for the evening, she couldn't resist a run down to the beach. She took off her Teva sandals and stepped to water's edge, allowing the cold liquid to play over the tops of her toes. The sand beneath her feet was cool and hard-packed, like a pour of just-smoothed concrete on which her footsteps would leave permanent imprints.

Yet thirty feet farther from the water, the sand softened into a wide, flat cushion whelked into ridges like the inside of a seashell by wind, and narrowing off to a single point where sand, sea, and ocean- horizon met. *That's what infinity looks like, she thought. The appearance of a point in time and space. But when we arrive there, nothing actually ends, it just continues.*

A few high clouds now hung over the horizon, tinged pink by the sun that'd inched closer to the water. Looking up and down the beach in both directions, it seemed amazing she had the area to herself. In summer this place would be popular with families camping and kids playing on the sand and splashing in the water. But now, in December, it might be the chill or the busyness of the season that kept most folks away.

Suddenly the deserted beach seemed as much an invitation to fill with thoughts as would the blank screen on her computer. Pulling away from the mesmerizing view, she climbed back up to her cabin, left her sandy Tevas by the front door, then set up her VAIO on the small desk. Though she'd scores of mobile offices over the years, this one seemed so quaint: a littoral setting for her literal, or literary endeavors. She smile at the word play, adjust the chair, and started writing.

What's been going on with me lately? Am I on course? Or did I get derailed somewhere? Sometimes I feel as if I'm floating, drifting back and forth in time. I sink into these deep dreams, then when I wake up I don't recall exactly where I was. I've been assuming this has to do with the head injury, but I don't really want to know, or I'd go get it looked at. And in any case, they'd likely just tell me it takes time to heal.

I think I need this short getaway, and this little cabin is perfect. In my own office, I get focused on work and it takes all my attention. But self-reflection? Not so much. So this is my chance.

If I'm honest with myself, I think my short-term memory is impaired. I've read this can happen to trauma victims. Things that happened last year, ten years ago, twenty, thirty . . . I have no problem remembering. But lately, all I can really remember clearly of recent events are my trips to lighthouses, my visit to Kuyama today, and my conversations with Delmar.

Deputy Johnson. Interesting guy. Part of me wants to march right up to him and ask why he seems to be so interested in me. And if he is, why doesn't he just call and schedule a meeting . . . or a cup of coffee . . . or even a date? When I'm with him, we're on exactly the same wave length. And then one of us leaves, and we have no plans to stay in touch or follow up.

And speaking of relationships . . . surely there must be other people I should be hearing from, or be in touch with. Yet, for the moment, I can't think of who they might be, so I just have to trust they'll call me if I'm supposed to be somewhere or do something.

People who don't call. They've always bothered me. Did that all start with him, the boy who didn't call back in college days?

Chris and her high school love had drifted apart after graduation, with Chris heading to Bronxville, New York, and Ron heading to Ithaca. Though still technically in the same state, the four-hour drive by car would only have been undertaken by people in a committed relationship, and theirs was no longer that.

Then, typical of Ron, he did show up at her Sarah Lawrence dorm one day, poised impatiently outside her locked room and looking at her as though she were late for an appointment. "What are you doing here?" she'd blurted, too startled to register the delight at seeing him. "Waiting for you," he'd said, switching his gaze from impatient to smoldering. That weekend they'd only left her room to make quick runs for food and water.

And then, he'd disappeared again, absorbed in his studies at Cornell, yes, but—she had no doubt—also pursued and pursuing other females. He'd been cute in high school. But in college, he'd come into his own, muscles sculpted, face chiseled, charm oozing. Whether he entered a small classroom or walked across the lobby of Grand Central Station, heads turned to look at him. He spent a quarter of his energy trying to escape all the attention.

A month had gone by—an eternity by college standards—when he did start calling and leaving messages with whoever happened to grab the one phone in her dorm's common room. Chris would get scribbled messages taped to her door. "Ron called." Getting him on the phone proved just as difficult, and she never knew whether her messages reached him.

One weekend, fed up with the lack of actual communication, and with the uncertainty of their "relation-ship," Chris headed for Port Authority and took the six-hour-plus bus ride to Ithaca. She disembarked at the foot of the long hill where Cornell was perched, and used the pay phone on the corner. She left a message with someone: "I'm here."

She settled into a booth in the diner at the foot of the hill, uncertain how many minutes, or hours, it'd be before he appeared. As it turned out, it didn't take long. She smiled when she saw his expression as he poked his head into the diner: first shock, then glee. That boded well for their weekend.

His dorm room window was draped in cotton fabric from India, as were his lamps, giving the space a mysterious, inviting aura. Incense perfumed the air. After taking her coat and inviting her to remove her boots, he ushered her to his one comfortable chair and said, "Listen."

Then he dropped the needle of his turntable on a Laura Nyro record. Chris felt herself transported by the singer's passionate offerings, by turns mournful and angry, tender and playful. And oh, was she ever romantic, from the depth of her soul, whether begging for Bill in her "Wedding Bell Blues" or serenading about a lovely afternoon in "Stone Soul Picnic."

Chris remembered that later, Nyro's songs had been recorded by one star after another, and that her music had influenced Joni Mitchell, Todd Rundgren, Carly Simon, Phoebe Snow, Elton John, and maybe others.

Chris had sensed that Nyro, like herself, had close friends and colleagues in the black community. Nyro grew up in the Bronx, and Chris in Compton, sharing schools and streets with people of color. Chris had heard it in Laura's music right away, a resonating soulful quality. Indeed, later on "Gonna Take a Miracle," another song Chris loved, Laura invited Patti LaBelle, Nona Hendryx and Sarah Dash to sing background.

But back in that moment, in the delicate, moody cocoon of Ron's college room, what had it meant that he'd played for her that sensitive, evocative artist? Chris had never tried to put it into words, nor had Ron. But the music had created for them a language as deep as their souls and as mutual as the air they breathed. So even though her career was built upon words, that moment with Ron had perhaps for the first time established for her a trust in communication beyond words.

Why am I thinking of that moment now? Is it because Del reminds me of Ron? I think he does. I've thought of it a couple of times before. They could be brothers: similar lines, though Delmar is maybe an inch shorter and more muscular. Didn't Ron have a brother? I dimly remember a "brat bro," a couple of years younger. I could ask Del . . . if we ever have a personal conversation. Will we?

Orange light tinged her desk and keyboard. She looked up and saw that it now painted the oceanscape in jewel tones. A band of ruby cut horizontally across her view, blending upward to topaz, then larimar, aquamarine, and sapphire. *Why am I thinking of gems?* She could only attribute the metaphors to the stunning inspiration of the sky.

Exhaustion tugged at her, and she had a long hike ahead of her tomorrow. She zipped herself into her sleeping bag and hoped for a peaceful night. She began to drift, thinking of how her life had changed. *Deadlines. I've lived my life by them. It feels so odd not to have one now.*

Delmar drove over the State Route 46 mountain pass and headed north on highway 1. The sinking sun promised a beautiful sunset. And even though daylight savings had recently begun and the days were growing longer, he wouldn't quite make it home in time, so he stopped off in Cambria and headed to Leffingwell Landing, a small state park at the north end of Moonstone Beach.

Often populated by locals who practiced ritual sunset viewing, today's bluster had left only a few visitors. Del parked at the far end, lowered both windows, and turned off his vehicle to enjoy the quiet and let the breeze blow through.

Had his entire life-view shifted today? Or was the eventful meeting at Kuyama's just a continuation, a confirmation, of what he'd always known?

A pastor in his mother's church had once discussed death with him, an all-too-frequent occurrence in the violent neighborhood of his youth. Though the pastor had neither white-washed not made excuses for the violence that only systemic change could quell, he also had a calm in the face of tragedy that Del found hard to grasp.

The pastor had looked him in the eye, then said, "You know, there's here. And there's here-after." Then he'd nodded and started a conversation with another parishioner. That phrase came back to Del now. 'Here. After.' As though when we died we didn't actually go anywhere. We were still here. After.

For the first time, that concept seemed to fit the facts, as he knew them. If Chris Christian was, in fact, a person who had died, and whose physical remains would show up one day, she herself seemed unaware of her own death. Did that mean she was in a sort of limbo, neither able to continue her earthly journey, nor ready to move on to whatever came next?

And if Chris was in "limbo" what would trigger her exit, her freedom to move forward? Was it part of his job to force her awareness? He saw no forcing on Kuyama's part, and the elder was the mentor to follow in this unknown territory. Apparently

Chris—or her spirit—trusted both Kuyama and him, and their requirement was to help her when, if, and how they could.

Suddenly famished, Del headed home and pulled a boxed entree out of his freezer, then popped it in the microwave. Lobster mac-and-cheese sounded almost decadently comforting. And that's what he needed this evening—comfort.

One more item in his freezer tempted him tonight: a small baguette that would take just a few minutes to bake. If he had a dietary downfall, it would be bread. In fact, if he succumbed to his impulses he'd be able to describe himself a panivorous.

Chuckling, he slid the loaf into the toaster over, which he set on 350 degrees, then reached into his fridge for a beer. Central Coast Brewing had been established recently in SLO and he'd decided to give it a try. Liking the idea of supporting a local business, he'd bought a few cans of their Deep Dark stout.

While the food heated, and the beer soothed his throat, he sat at his table and looked through Chris Christian's notebook to confirm the lighthouse stamps he'd previously seen. All three were there: Piedras Blancas, Point Vicente, and Point San Luis.

When his dinner was ready, he carried it to the living room and watched some news as he ate, savoring the rich, buttery flavor of the pasta, and enjoying the hot, crusty bread.

April 1997 had its share of interesting stories. According to the talking head on Del's TV screen the U.S. Appeals Court upheld the constitutionality of California's Preference Ban, which ruled that voters had the right to forbid use of racial and gender-based preferences in affirmative action programs. Next, the Whitewater inquiry hit the news again with James McDougal getting a 3-year Sentence for illegally obtaining millions in federally backed loans.

The best news of the day confirmed the U.S. economy had grown at its fastest pace in nine years and Clinton's administration predicted the deficit would soon be reduced to $75 billion, its lowest in 20 years. And maybe most interesting was that a 21-year-old Black-Asian golfer set a new Masters record. Young Tiger Woods won at Augusta, by 12 strokes.

Somehow the news of the day, even the negative stories, made him feel his feet were back on the ground, rather than hanging in mid-air. Talking to ghosts, waking-dreams, and theories about missing persons receded at least as far as the back row of his mental theatre.

With some of his sense of normalcy restored, Del washed his dishes, turned off the lights and headed to bed.

Chapter 17

Chris woke in her tiny cabin, aware that her body felt toasty warm, but her nose was as cold as brass. December in an ocean-side shelter was no picnic.

To stay warm, she'd either have to spend the day zipped into her down bag, or get up, get dressed, and start moving around. She quickly availed herself of the icy facilities and pulled on the silk long underwear she'd packed, then layered on jeans and a jersey top. Adding her fleece jacket, she stepped onto the balcony for a moment. Where the beach view had offered a cyclorama light show last evening, at dawn the water glowed a delicate silver that blended into a pearlescent gray sky.

She went back inside, locked the slider, and checked the provisions in her backback: two water bottles, a couple of granola bars, an apple, extra socks, small camera, mini-cassette recorder, a powerful flashlight with extra batteries and, of course, her notebook.

This was her bundle—her jalama. In her reading, she'd discovered the meaning of the Chumash word, named after the original village of Xalam that'd served as a midpoint between the coast and the inland village. People passing through carried their bundles.

I'm better prepared today than I was at the Clarke house. The memory fragment hit her like a sharp hail stone. But she swept it away and let it melt.

Properly outfitted for her hike, she locked the cabin's front door and checked the doors of her SUV. With the air so decidedly chilly, she kept on her fleece jacket, then put her arms through the straps of her backpack. She sat on the cabin's front step to dust sand from her feet, then pulled on her socks and laced up her boots. In the process, she glanced down and noticed a sand dollar sitting to the side of her cabin's entrance. *The second one I've found!*

It seemed a good omen, and she zipped the little talisman in her pocket, then set off southward toward the lighthouse.

Chris used the Jalama Creek estuary as her starting point and walked for an hour before stopping for a sip of water. On more solid terrain she might move along at three miles per hour, but on this sandy soil, she figured she might cover more like two. That put her about halfway to the point, which was now in view. Warm enough, now, she removed her fleece, put it inside her pack, then put her arms back into the straps. Low tide would occur at about 9:30, and since she'd left the cabin a little at 7:00, she expected her timing to be about right.

Sure enough, another hour farther south she arrived at the sedimentary shale layered downward from the lighthouse to the beach floor. Surveying the scant toeholds on the stack-stones, she knew she could never scale them. But now she looked for the narrow dirt path that'd be visible, and accessible, only with the tide this low. With relief, she spotted it, took a breath, then began to climb.

She now was entering truly unknown territory. Jalama State Park was, of course, public property. So was Gaviota State Park, a south-facing property around the end of the point, where the coastline changed direction. But in between, where she now climbed, she would cross into the private property that surrounded the lighthouse land and might have no visible demarcation, given the remote location and difficult access. That didn't mean she wouldn't encounter a guard—or even a guard dog. In the case of the former, she'd beg ignorance; all she could do about the latter was hope to bonk it on the head with her heavy flashlight. She had never heard anything about a canine guard, and she figured she had a way with human ones. *We journalists often go where we're not wanted, not invited, and not welcome. Part of the job.*

If a person loved wild places—and Chris did—this location held treasures. A sanctuary for wildlife including bald eagles and peregrine falcons, the steep cliffs revealed geological pre-history with marine sediments upthrust in ancient seismic events. Vertical arroyos cut by streams angled sharply from the 500-foot peaks down to the sea. *Not a good place to fall.* As if she needed reminding.

The dirt path was really an old road, rutted by winter rains and constant wind, covered with shale that slipped out from under her boots. But she continued climbing the hill until she crested on the coastal mountain above the lighthouse.

She took a deep breath and surveyed the most extraordinary view she'd ever seen: 300 degrees of coast and ocean. Away to the east stretched the south-facing Santa Barbara coastline. To the north, Jalama itself was no longer visible, but beyond it, the land's lineation extended off to infinity.

From this vantage, she could clearly see this as a transition point. The abrupt northward turn of the land might be the clearest visual, but from what she read, the unseen currents clashing below the surface were even more dramatic, posing a threat to navigation, and sometimes even called the Cape Horn of the Pacific. This was the end of the southern waters and the start of the northern, as exhibited by shifts in everything from climate to species.

She sensed the line of demarcation as something more, an almost tangible cleavage. Seismic, yes. But also psychic? Or a rift in time/space? Perhaps that's what made it the Western Gate that Kuyama spoke about. A crack in the physical universe where the spiritual shown through?

She glanced down toward the water. Interestingly, the light-house itself was not above her present location, but below it. She remembered that it'd been moved so as to be visible below the fog that often collected at the point.

She followed the steep staircase that led down, counting all 180 steps as she descended, till she stood next to the remaining historic structures. Indeed, buildings had come and gone over the years since 1856, when the original lighthouse had been constructed. Now, the two primary buildings were a cylindrical tower and a wide, stucco rectangle that stood in front of it a though protecting the tower from the sea, while allowing the lens itself to appear over top of its orange roof. The black-framed lens room supported a green cap, and Chris could imagine that when the iceplant ground-cover erupted into pinks in spring, the whole point would be vibrantly colorful.

Having come this far, she walked toward the narrow entranceway of the rectangular building and tried the door. Once again to her surprise, she found it unlocked, and stepped into the cool, dim interior. Her nostrils expanded at the scent, now famil-iar from the other lighthouse visits, but much stronger, given the closed and deserted premises. The olfactory signature contained notes of both decay and freshness: seaweed and mildew, damp wood and musty concrete, hillside loam, and lingering wood-smoke leftover from long-ago cookstove fires and a faint metallic bite from its scorched iron.

The empty rooms didn't yield much visually, but the sounds echoing in the space seemed to travel right through her. At first, she attributed the reverberations to the surf pounding the cliff below. Moans interlaced the percussive crashes, which she figured must be wind whistling through the eaves. And yet it began to sound like voices.

How many souls had drowned at this point? Twenty-three sailors died here in 1923: the largest peacetime loss of U.S. Navy ships when seven destroyers ran aground just north of here. In 1917, though this incident only resulted in one death, the Coast Guard Cutter McCulloch sank when it collided in the fog with the passenger steamship SS Governor. The earliest shipwreck off the point that she remembered reading about was the Yankee Blade. In 1854 a gang of pirates boarded her in San Francisco then ran her aground between Points Conception and Arguello to gain its cargo of gold bullion. The ill-fated voyage resulted in published accounts of a reign of terror, and the deaths of many.

Every lighthouse is built for a reason, usually as the result of a disaster. Could she be hearing the mournful cries of those who were never rescued? Or hundreds and even thousands of years earlier, could this have been a burial site for the Chumash? *Is that why they call is the Western Gate?*

Suddenly the fog horn sounded. Had its deep single tone been carried away by the wind till now? The sound brought to mind the science fiction author Ray Bradbury's *The Fog Horn* about a monster from the sea who climbs up to try to mate with the lighthouse. And thinking of sea monsters, she could now imagine why the corny old 1959 Sci-Fi movie *The Monster of Piedras Blancas* had actually been filmed not at the real Piedras lighthouse, but here.

Why do I always remember film scenes? She could theorize it was the result of so many years of video producing, but she knew the ability had been with her long before. The eponymous monster came to mind, strangely terrifying even in the hokey costume, as bad as a child's packaged Halloween outfit complete with rubber mask and fins.

Then, sure enough, scenes from the film began to flash through her mind, with the authenticity of the location overcoming the corn-ball fish-man suit. Clear panes of glass surrounding the enormous first-order Fresnel; the staircase spiraling down from the lens; Lucy, dutiful daughter of the lighthouse keeper, the pro-verbial damsel-in-distress when the monster breaks into the keeper's home and carries her off to the dangerous cliff. *This very building, and that very cliff,* Chris reminded herself, a little shiver tracing over her skin.

The movie built to its climax as the monster climbs the light tower and hurls the lightkeeper to his death; the hero's own rope-climb to the top where he shoves the monster away to crash into the water; then the lovers in the clinches as the revolving Fresnel shines out onto the dark sea.

Chris pulled herself away from the fanciful imagery to explore the rooms, finding neither the cozy kitchen of Point San Luis, nor the glass cases of Piedras Blancas. Instead, this location had a truly deserted quality, as though visitors were no longer welcome.

Finally, on the floor of an otherwise empty closet, she found a cardboard box containing an inkpad, pieces of scrap paper, and a dried-out stamp. *Someone couldn't bear to throw this away. Well, might as well use it.* Withdrawing the notebook from her backpack, she flipped to a blank page, pressed the stamp several times into the inkpad, and did her best to make an impression.

Her mission, such as it was, seemed complete here. Aside from a spectacular view and some leftover movie moments, she had little to show for it. She went out through the same door, surprised to see the sun was already lowering toward the horizon. *Must've lost track of time in there.* She also realized she'd missed her window to walk back to Jalama in daylight, as the rising tide had overtaken the lower pathway. Her next chance would come at about midnight. She had some time to kill.

Delmar tossed and turned when he should have been enjoying REM sleep. As though straddling a deck that bounded over the waves, he rode an unfamiliar ship determined to protect his shipmates. But then the ship tossed him overboard like a toy and he woke in mid-air.

Startled and gasping, he steadied himself on the edge of the bed, glancing around the room for remnants of the ghostly images, but saw none. His digital clock glowed 12:00 in red numerals.

Midnight. On the shortest day.

Why was he thinking of winter solstice now, during spring? *Something Kuyama mentioned?* No, he'd have remembered that, and that'd be a day she'd spend with other members of her community for ceremony. *Then it must've been part of my dream.*

And Chris had been bound for Point Conception next, where there've been shipwrecks through the years. Is that why I had that nightmare?

Though he'd gone to bed a few hours earlier feeling more peaceful, now his concerns were stirred again, and he wasn't sure why. But usually, when a case wouldn't leave him alone, it generally meant a clue was trying to rise up through his consciousness . . . a clue, something overlooked, a detail missed.

He knew he couldn't possibly get back to sleep at this point, so he stepped into his slippers and headed downstairs. He wished he had a bag of that tea Kuyama had served earlier, but he found some P.G. Tipps, a particularly strong British blend, that'd help him stay awake for a while.

He sat again at his dining table, spreading out his notes, files, and Chris's notebook. This was how he'd approach any normal case, with line-by-line grunt work. *Not that there's anything else normal about this case.*

The unexpected thoughts about solstice suggested that he review dates and times. He didn't know what he'd be looking for, but trusted the guidance these intuitions provided.

First, he printed out blank calendar pages starting last Halloween—the date of the first lighthouse visit stamp in Chris's notebook. With sheets for October 1996 through the current month, April 1997, laid out on his table, he began jotting in details.

> 10-31-96 Piedras Blancas lighthouse visit
> 11-11-96 Point Vicente lighthouse visit
> 11-21-96 Point San Luis lighthouse visit
> 4-7-97 Point Conception lighthouse visit (if she kept
> to her plan.)

There was quite a gap between those last two visits, he noticed. He studied the sheets for another moment trying to determine whether anything special about those dates caught his attention.

Yes! It's right in front of me! He suddenly realized the first three visits all fell on holidays: Halloween, Veteran's Day, and Thanksgiving.

Really? What a sad commentary, if Chris had nothing better to do than visit a lighthouse, when virtually everyone visited with family or friends? Or was this actually typical of her, so focused on whatever might be her current work project that she made no time for friendships?

When had he interviewed Joseph Calvin the night of his party? Referring to his own day planner from the previous year, he saw that'd taken place December 13th. *Did I actually see Chris that night? Or was that one of my dreams?* Just in case, he added the date to the December worksheet.

When they had met yesterday with Kuyama, Chris was clearly fascinated by Chumash culture, which included celebrating winter solstice. Technically, that would be the next holiday, the shortest day of the year. And about two weeks later came perihelion, when Earth would be closest to the sun. Were these important?

Maybe there's something about it in her notebook. He opened it, realizing he'd perused it several times, but not carefully gone through it page by page from the beginning. He'd do that soon. For now, he riffled through till he found the Point San Luis stamp, imagining there might be notes about Kuyama after that.

But what he saw made his hand spasm as though he'd received an electric shock. There it was: the stamp that had not been there the night before. The impression was so faint, it was hard to see. He brought the notebook up closer to the light that overhung the table. Point Conception Light. 12-21-96.

She visited the fourth lighthouse last December. But I saw her yesterday, and she hadn't yet gone to Point Conception. Del began to tremble, as he'd seen Chris do on both previous visits. He began to feel light-headed, as though he might pass out, and he clutched the edge of the table, lowered his head and closed his eyes.

Then his emergency training kicked in. *Treat this like any other urgent situation. Assess. Check the facts. Breathe.* As his pulse began to settle, logic began to return. Just because her dates didn't match his, didn't mean he couldn't figure this out.

According to her calendar, she visited Kuyama on December 20th. Yet according to *his* calendar—the real world calendar — she had been there with him yesterday, April 6, 1997. And when had they talked about her adoption piece in the video room? That'd happened in March.

Could two timelines occur side by side? The law of relativity proved two people could experience the passage of time in two completely different ways. But could Chris's actually be called a time line? It seemed to be functioning more like a series of loops. Maybe tides was a more apt metaphor— something she had mentioned as they sat at the table in Atascadero yesterday.

What if, for the sake of argument, he totally accepted that Chris was detached from the calendar of terra firma, and was somehow free-floating in time? From his perspective, she'd appear to be jumping over normal chronology. But from her perspective, time might even appear normal.

From his point of view, Chris seemed to be traveling both forward and backward in time. She had traveled forward to meet at Kuyama's; but evidently she'd traveled backward to be at the Calvin party. So maybe she really wasn't there, though his memory of seeing her was clear.

I might need a new definition of "really." She could, indeed, have been there, even if no one saw her but me. So if she was at Calvin's party—but no one else saw her—she must already have been dead by then. What if all her lighthouse "visits" happened posthumously? What's the last known date anyone—other than Kuyama and I—actually saw her?

Was she at the Calvin party? He could certainly ask Joseph Calvin. But he knew what the man would say. He'd say that, by then, Chris had been missing for several weeks. He'd say Chris had known there would be a party for his son that night, but that he hadn't heard from her.

He may as well work through *her* calendar. And he did have specific dates when either from her day planner, her notes or known contest. With the amended dates, he now wrote a new list:

10-19-96 Day planner notation - Clarke house to meet
contact
10-31-96 Halloween - Piedras Blancas lighthouse visit
11-11-96 Veteran's Day - Point Vicente
lighthouse visit
11-21-96 Thanksgiving - Point Luis lighthouse visit
12-13-96 Joseph Calvin party - Santa Barbara
12-21-96 Winter Solstice - Point Conception visit
3-20-97 Equinox - meets with me to review VCR tapes
4-6-97 Meeting with Kuyama and me, Atascadero

Chris said she had files for me in her car. She arrived after I did, so I didn't see her drive up, and in fact have never seen her car. But from her perspective, she's still driving it. Does that mean that if I find her car, I'll find her . . . or her remains?

Chapter 18

Chris had left the lonely confines of the lighthouse building to climb into the light tower itself. Though she'd recently been inside the housing for the Point Vicente's tower with its Third order Fresnel, Point Conception housed a First order, which was nearly twice the height of the Third. The lamp itself towered over her and was nearly six feet in diameter.

Magnificently faceted, it turned like a diamond being shown off in a jeweler's window, if that jeweler were a giant with a gem to match. The size qualified this as a hyperradiant lens, and indeed its beam would be visible twenty miles out to sea.

Without staring too long into its brightness, Chris remembered her research. The Fresnel lens, named for its French inventor, reduced the amount of material required compared to a conventional lens by dividing the lens into a set of concentric annular sections. It could capture more oblique light from a source, and produced a collimated, or parallel set of beams, both of which qualities made it visible over greater distances.

At the horizon, an orange glow lingered but offered little illumination to the seascape below. But a bright planet was just winking on in the darkening sky. She began to feel drowsy, realizing it'd already been a long day, and that once the tide went out again, she'd have another long hike. *Maybe I should take a short nap.*

Leaning her head against the large, mullioned window, she looked out from her high perch. Against the dark water, she began to notice the carefully lighted structures of off-shore oil rigs laid out like jeweled brooches on a field of black satin.

I wrote an article about off-shore rigs a long time ago. I thought I'd hate them, but they're amazing . . . floating cities that support underwater ecosystems. At night, they look like diamonds. Crystal ships . . . wasn't there a song?

The Doors . . . Jim Morrison . . . on the "Light My Fire" album. It came back to her then, and she begun humming, remembering a lyric here and there. "Before you slip into unconsciousness . . . Another flashing chance at bliss. . . ."

A flashing chance at bliss. That's all we get, isn't it? Here, with the lighthouse beam flashing past her and over the water, she considered again . . . that long ago time with Ron.

Morrison's haunting vocal floated up to her as though rising from the distant lights of the sparkling platforms. "We'll meet again. . ." But would they? Where was he now? Married and settled, happy in an entirely different life. "The crystal ship is being filled. . . ." *By someone else, not by me.*

He'd married a super model, become a photographer, created an international life of glamour and success. *But he embarked on that life without knowing how I felt. Why? What held me back? Was I such a repressed female that I waited for him to share first?*

If she'd been able to birth that child so long ago and had a daughter now, what would she tell her? *Speak your mind. Then speak your heart.* Chris had never had much trouble with the former. It was the latter that'd proved not only difficult, but impossible.

No longer sleepy, and too disturbed by morose thoughts to stay put, Chris rose, descended the spiral staircase, and stepped out into the blustery night, waiting a moment for her eyes to adjust to the darkness.

Strangely, the light from the Fresnel seemed to be extending its reach beyond what it had a moment ago, its powerful beams reaching upward toward the Milky Way, outward across the water, and downward to where she stood.

But the light isn't designed to illuminate the terrain. This makes no sense. Is the lens damaged? Did I lean too much on the window? Confusion and alarm tingled down her synapses, and then the blast of the fog horn strummed through her as if she were a bass fiddle.

As she looked upward, the beams of light continued to expand, and now seemed to be accompanied by a cloud of some sort. She backed away from the structure, but then looked behind her, realizing she was perilously close to the escarpment.

I can't run down . . . I'll have to run up! The long exterior stairway that led up the steep hill now seemed the only means of escaping the cloud. Pearlescent and illuminated by the lighthouse beams, the cloud nevertheless had a dark heart that seemed aimed directly at her. *If I'm engulfed in that thing, I won't be able to see anything. I'll fall! I don't want to fall again!*

She clambered up the stairs as quickly as her legs would carry her, barely moving faster than the advancing microburst. The odor of ozone tingled in her nostrils. Had the storm advanced across the water? She hadn't noticed any kind of weather anomaly. In fact, the cloud seemed to be emanating from the Fresnel itself!

Once she made it to the hilltop, a crested ridge rose higher and farther away from the cloud. Without stopping to consider any other options, she scrambled up the slope, watching her feet, lest she trip over the oatgrass or slip on the sedimentary shale.

Exhaustion tugged at her thighs and burned through her lungs. She clutched at bunched grasses as she climbed, only to find herself holding green ribbons that were instantly swept away by the howling wind of the storm.

Up ahead, she saw a glimmer of light. *A structure? Headlights?* Whatever it was, it might offer shelter and she summoned a final burst of energy to get to it. She dared glance backward, and could see past the storm, which suddenly began to contract around the light tower, then fade as though it'd never been there at all.

Chris stood, took a long moment to catch her breath, then felt for her backpack, which still hung from her shoulders. She hesitated to descend the hill immediately, lest some trace of the storm return. So instead, she continued upward, toward the light she'd seen.

As she approached, a small campfire came into focus, surrounded by a group of people sitting around a fire. *A fire? Among these wild grasses? Surely that's not permitted.*

Now she faced another conundrum. If they'd seen her, would they assume she'd report them? Would they come after her? Chase her back down the dangerous slope? *I can't outrun them in the dark. Better just bluster forward.*

As she came closer, the group seemed calm, even somber. They stared at their fire, not at her. And now she saw they all appeared to be Native American. *Oh, no! I'm stumbling into a ceremony!* They sat around the perimeter of a circle of stones—a sacred circle, if she could read the scene.

"Uh, I—" she stuttered. "I apologize. I don't mean to disturb you."

One of the men looked up. "You're welcome to join us," he said, his tone a bit stilted, but the words far friendlier than what she'd expected.

"Oh, no, I don't want to intrude, I—"

"It's no intrusion for those who are seeking," a woman said.

Unsure what subtle meaning underlay her invitation, Chris now felt it would be rude just to ignore their gathering and continue on her way. "Thank you," she said, standing awkwardly in the dark beyond the glow of their light.

"Come into the circle. Have a seat," offered the woman.

There were four members of the group, and Chris made the fifth. She sat cross-legged on the ground in a space that'd apparently been left empty. *Almost as though they were expecting one more person.*

"Long journey," said one of the men. It didn't seem to be a question, but Chris confirmed it with a nod.

"Water?" the woman asked.

"I have some, thanks," Chris replied, slipping out of her back-pack and retrieving her bottle from its zippered compartment.

While they sat in companionable silence, Chris observed her new acquaintances more carefully. Two men, two women, wearing jeans and fleeces—like herself—but also sporting long hair and carrying the carved features and graceful lines of some of the Chumash people she'd met. "Are you," she ventured, "observing a special occasion here?"

The four looked at one another, then the first man said, "A ceremony."

Chris nodded, though his answer hadn't really clarified what ceremony it might be. She followed their persistent gaze toward the fire, noticing for the first time that a pattern was drawn in the sandy dirt. A five-pointed design had been carefully drawn, looking something like a sand dollar.

She wished she could take out her flashlight to inspect the drawing better, but didn't dare disturb their ceremony with such an encroachment. Instead, she peered at it more closely. It is a sand dollar, she realized: five elongated, toothed openings began at the central fire, then extended outward; and each ended where a notch would be, represented here by seashells. Are those actual sand dollars? They were. But the one at her place was missing. From her pocket she withdrew her own sand dollar and placed it to match the others.

Soft mumbles rose from all the others around the circle and Chris enjoyed a sense of approval. Then, she suddenly felt overcome with fatigue, a strange lassitude rapidly overtaking her limbs.

"This is a good place to rest," the woman said.

Taking her at her word, Chris angled her legs to one side, stretched her upper body to the other and rested her head on her backpack.

The drum beat started first, then the deep voice lifted in a melodic strain. It was one of the men from the sacred circle, now dressed

elaborately in feathers and fur, and displaying beautifully painted designs on his brown skin.

The circle no longer surrounded a fire, and he stepped into its center, beating on his hand-hewn drum and singing. Then he began to speak about the bear representing the strength of the mother, and the eagle representing a time of reflection.

Chris heard the unmistakable peal and looked up to see a huge eagle circling overhead. Then she heard a rustle in nearby bushes, and felt neither fear nor surprise at noticing the hulking shape of a bear.

"This is a time," the man continued, "to remember our loved ones that we carry in our hearts as we lose them through the years . . . a time to make choices for the future."

Whose future? *Chris wondered.* It's as if they're talking to me. The ceremony honors four points. But the sand dollar has five. Does the fifth represent time? Seems like it might.

". . . the time of a new sun . . . the winter solstice, the time of the rains and the winds."

Winter solstice. That's today! That's the ceremony I wandered into!

The man blew on a conch shell and he faced the east, back along the coastline toward Santa Barbara. He's going to face each of the cardinal points. *His words continued, ". . . where the sun rises. . . ."*

When he blew on the conch shell again, he faced south, mentioning the snake and the owl, the summer, our youth and our vision. He spoke about summer as the time of respect and energy. And he spoke of it as a time for authors. Perhaps he really is speaking to me!

Again, he blew on the conch and faced west, where she'd seen the sun sink into the ocean, and seen the storm rise. He called it a time when day ends and dreams begin.

Yes, this is where I am. Day has ended. And I keep dreaming. I'm never sure any more whether I'm awake or asleep, but if this is a dream, it's bringing me the information I need.

"...a time of transition," the speaker said, "where the ocean and the land meet."

What would the fourth direction signify? The deep, hollow sound of the conch rose a final time and he spoke about winter, many cultures, and how much we have to teach one another. And he spoke of Houtache, Mother Earth, where we lay our loved ones to rest.

Birth. Death. And everything in between. "To everything there is a season." That's how the Bible expressed it. And every indigenous or ancient culture she'd visited through the years held ceremonies recognizing the cardinal points. Though the wisdom expressed here on this mountainside was not new, it was primordial, and she felt it seep into her bones. When she focused again on the speaker, she heard his final words: "To see dreams come true."

Chris awoke from the dream to find herself still sitting in the fire circle. "This is a Winter Solstice ceremony, isn't it?" she asked, already knowing the answer.

"It is," said the woman who'd spoken earlier. "But it is also a ceremony for someone who is on their way into spirit."

"You mean they died?"

"Yes," the man said after a pause.

"But the soul lingers until it's ready to go," the woman added.

Chris breathed for another moment, then said, "I'm sorry for your loss. Is there . . . something appropriate I could say or do in honor of your friend?"

"Just join us in knowing that her spirit will find its way," one of them replied.

"I will. Is there something special about this location?"

"Yes. This is the Western Gate."

Chris began to shudder, as she had a few times recently, though she wasn't aware of a sudden chill. *The Western Gate! What Kuyama explained. So this is exactly where I was supposed to come! Does that mean . . . was she trying to tell me . . . am I . . .?*

"When your time comes, you can come here." The female voice reached to her from the fireside, though she couldn't see either of the women's faces.

"My time? Oh! I see. Well, thank you. But I . . . I have some really important things I still have to do."

Chris left the circle abruptly. After a few steps, she'd plunged into darkness, so she stopped to withdraw her flashlight and slide her arms through the straps of her backpack.

After hurriedly making sure the ocean was to her left, she began her descent. At first, all she could hear were the arguments in her own thought. She took offence at the woman saying "when your time comes." *How dare she! Reminds me of when my banker told me I should make out my will. And I was only forty at the time!* "But your job is risky, wouldn't you say?" the banker had asked. And Chris had shoved aside the advice, knowing there was plenty of time for that.

But as she watched the beam from her flashlight bounce over the rugged, descending trail back to the beach, her thoughts calmed and she realized she had, in fact, made some arrangements.

For one thing, she'd worked with an estate planner. She didn't have jewels, or expensive furniture. But she had a nice condo worth quite a bit in the California real estate market. She'd made arrangements for the proceeds of its sale to start a scholarship fund for investigative journalism.

For another, she'd been cataloging her assignments over the years as though they mattered, as though she had something to leave for others. The most valuable thing she'd leave behind were her notes, and the scene-by-scene descriptions of how her major assignments had unfolded. *There it is again, that predilection I have for seeing things in cinematic scenarios. In fact, wait'll I write about today!*

She neared the bottom of the long escarpment. While the lighthouse beam spotlighted the coastline high overhead, her smaller beam slid over the terrain below her. The tide had, indeed, gone out again, and she was safe to continue.

As her feet touched down on the hard-packed sand, and she retraced the 4-mile hike back to her rented cabin, she put her hand into her fleece pocket and remembered she'd left the sand dollar in the fire circle.

I really used it as a sand "dollar" I think . . . as though it was payment for attending their ceremony.

She indulged in a long word-play, one of her favorite pastimes, and a good distraction during her long walk.

Payment . . . pay . . . how many ways could the word be used? Pay attention. Pay it forward. Offering payment implies the thing paid for has value. So it's a token. A token of validation, valuation, that says "I hear you, I value you, I see you."

In Greek mythology, those who died had to pay to cross the River Styx. The Bible said one must "pay the utmost farthing."

Was it payment of your final debt in life?

And here was another to play with: conception. There was its intellectual or literary meaning: the forming or devising of a plan or idea. This was the starting point for every writer, conceiving the idea for the story, the script, the book, the article. Indeed, it would be the inception point for any creative or business endeavor. It meant origination, genesis, the beginning of the beginning. And this is where the land began.

Meanwhile there were other meanings, both biological and religious. The second Spanish explorer to round the point had named the area Punta de la Limpia Concepcin, Point of the Immaculate Conception, referring to the Catholic view of the Virgin Mary.

And the biological definition referred to the moment a sperm fertilized an egg and began the mitotic magic of cell division and reproduction.

So this controversial, dangerous, majestic, imposing, intriguing and complex location was a nexus point for primordial, cultural, historical, and geographic elements. For the European-Americans, it represented where life begins. For the Native-American Chumash this was the Western Gate where life ends.

And what tied the two together? The sand dollar, which in itself was a physical representation of a nexus, defined as a connection or series of connections linking two or more things. It was a Christian symbol representing Christ's wounds. It was a symbol of conception. And it was the symbol for the Western Gate.

One more word came to mind. Biologically, a sand dollar body was a "test."

If all this was a test, did I pass?

High on the point above the lighthouse, the Chumash people prepared to conclude their gathering.

They carefully doused their fire, scattered the cool ashes and rubbed the dirt to remove such elements of the design as weren't already removed by wind and droplets of rain.

"She's not ready yet," said one of the men.

One of the women said, "We'll be here when she is."

Chapter 19

Chris woke refreshed in the little cabin, whose walls were tinged with pale first light. The now familiar chill might have encouraged her to stay cozy in her sleeping bag and try for another hour or two of sleep. But after her unusual adventure of the day and night before, she felt it was time to vacate her temporary digs. She might return to the Western Gate at some point, but for now she wanted to leave.

She had, however, enjoyed writing in a space other than her own office, and had decided she deserved consecutive getaways. She dressed, packed her car, then glanced around fondly at the cozy chamber. She might indeed return here for another respite sometime. The location was a gem.

Morning light hadn't yet crested over the mountains to the east as she made her way back to the 101 and headed north. With Christmas just days away, holiday lights still shone dimly in the wintery dawn, lending a festive air to the passing landscape.

She stopped at her condo long enough to swap clothes, grab her portable printer and a few files, then got back on the road to continue northward.

Though she'd made no actual vacation plans, she'd left a voice mail reserving a room at the Belhaven Inn on Touchstone Beach in Milford-Haven. The proprietors knew her, as she'd stayed there before, always staying in their upstairs corner room where she could write uninterrupted within view of the Piedras light, where she'd started her recent visits.

She scarcely noticed the passage of miles, or time, as she exited toward Highway 1 through SLO, hugging the coastline past Morro Bay and Cayucos, then taking the turnoff for Cambria.

Main Street seemed to be playing host to unusual visitors who stood in costumed groups. To her left, a group of nuns silently sang outside a local church; to her right, Edward Scissorhands stood ready to slice; at the edge of a side street, a minstrel strummed a silent guitar, and across from them Mr. & Mrs. Farmer held pitchforks beside a miniature tractor. Princesses and dragons, musical theatre stars and diners at bistro tables adorned the sidewalks. And in the middle of town, two terrifying cyclists pursued a tricyclist, all three pairs of legs pumping with electrical assistance.

So creative! Well, Cambria and Milford-Haven are artist towns, after all. But scarecrows are for autumn. Isn't it winter? She looked up in time to see a banner advertising the Cambria "Scarecrow Festival, Oct 1 - 31." *So it is autumn, not winter! And why have I never heard about this festival?*

After enjoying a few more views of the colorful characters, Chris remembered she'd picked up her mail at home. There hadn't been much, mostly junk fliers she'd stuffed into her briefcase to review later. But there was an oversized postcard sent by a gallery in Milford-Haven. The featured art work was by an artist she liked—Miranda Jones. And the artist's studio address was listed on the card. *As long as I'm doing some artistic sight-seeing, why not stop by her studio?*

Chris indulged this next whimsy, traveling a few miles closer to her accommodations, but climbing up a steep hill to the artist's place before heading down to her beach motel. After parking on the side of the narrow street, she stepped out and noticed a walkway that led around the side of the building to the back. A sweet balcony clung to the hillside and she stepped onto it. It did offer a winking view of ocean through the pines, but Chris instead peered inside the French doors that would open into the studio. With two walls made of windows, it was easy to see inside. *There's someone resting on that corner daybed. Must be the artist, but I don't want to disturb her.*

She examined the spacious room. Overhead beams of light oak crossed the high ceiling and matched the polished hardwood floor. On the far wall a clerestory window brought in northern light. Under it, several large paintings were hung, and a deep, wide cabinet held shallow trays for prints. Under the near row of windows stood the artist's desk, swept clean of debris, overhung with good lighting, and with a rolling chair tucked under it. An easel held a painting Chris couldn't see, and a row of glass bottles held an elaborate array of brushes of every size.

How must it feel to stand in this space, surrounded by natural beauty but empty inside except for tools of the trade? I bet facing that easel feels a lot like staring at a blank piece of paper. Maybe all creatives have in common this summoning, this listening, that must precede embarkation into any project.

Chris would have loved to step inside, take a guided tour, then interview the artist out here on the charming deck. But the black cat in the window didn't seem to approve, Miranda Jones seemed to be resting now, and Chris turned to other plans.

Miranda Jones woke from a nap on her studio daybed, unsure what had awakened her, but certain that something had.

She lay perfectly still for a long moment, listening for whatever noise didn't belong. While she listened, she remembered that, just before her nap, she'd opened a letter from the Lompoc Chamber of Commerce. They were inviting her to create a mural that would depict their main street, but also the nearby Point Conception Lighthouse. She'd always wanted to know more about the remote coastal town, and delighted at the prospect. She'd be in touch with them soon to review timing, budget, and to plan a preliminary visit.

Suddenly, she heard the noise that'd likely wakened her—Shadow hissing. Miranda gave a slight smile to the empty room, knowing her cat's protective nature. If a raccoon dared step onto the deck railing, or an opossum make himself comfortable in a tree too close to the house, Shadow expressed her outrage by hissing, growling, and sometimes even swiping at a window or sliding door, if glass separated her from the intruder.

Miranda shot her legs out from under the throw and headed into the adjacent living room to see whether she could spot their uninvited guest. But when she saw her black kitty in full alarm-mode, back rounded and every hair on end, she feared they might have a much larger problem. *A puma? A bobcat? A burglar?*

"Shadow, who is it?" She asked in a soothing tone, partly to conceal her own concern.

"Weowwww," Shadow moaned deep in her throat.

It didn't seem wise to open the door to the deck without knowing who or what might be lurking out there. So Miranda returned to the studio, where she could get a better angled view. She saw nothing and no one.

But since her cat continued to carry on, Miranda considered making a call to the Sheriff's department. Milford-Haven had no police department, but Deputy Delmar Johnson had been assigned to the region and actually lived here himself. Maybe he'd come by, if he had time.

Because they'd gradually become friends over the past few months, she decided she could contact him without making this an emergency call out, so rather than dialing 911, she used his local office.

"Deputy Johnson," he answered on the second ring.

"Deputy . . . uh, Delmar, this is Miranda Jones. Do you have a minute?:

"I do. What's up? You okay?"

"I am, yes. But there might be an intruder outside. I can't see anyone but my cat thinks it's hair-raising—literally —whoever or whatever it is."

"I'm not in town at the moment," he said, "but I can get back in fifteen minutes and I'll take a look around. Meanwhile, stay inside, and if you see or hear anything else, dial 911. There might be another officer closer than I am."

"Okay, Delmar. I doubt it's anything more than a raccoon, but I appreciate your swinging by."

"Got it. See you soon, and keep me posted."

Relieved that Delmar would be here soon, Miranda returned to Shadow, who had calmed somewhat, though she still emitted a soft growl. "It's okay kitty, nothing will hurt you." She bent to pick her up, and since Shadow allowed this, Miranda knew the cat's fears were allayed to some degree.

"You are such a good kitty," Miranda continued. "Thanks for protecting us. You're doing a good job." Stroking the top of Shadow's head, Miranda cooed further praise and endearments, until she asked, "Would you like a treat?"

With that, Shadow gave her short vocalization for "yes," leapt merrily to the floor, and headed toward the kitchen.

Chapter 20

Chris had slept well, then written all morning. But now she felt as restless as the leaves skittering down the lane outside her motel room. She'd been drawn to Milford-Haven for an additional getaway, feeling a need to compose her thoughts.

Writing had always been her tool, her method of processing and understanding her way through one experience after another. She'd often felt she wrote her way forward, one word, one article, one assignment at a time.

She'd come up with a kind of slogan for her work along the way, something she first remembered discussing with her mentor Reed years earlier. In the afterglow of the Apollo Soyuz mission, they'd had dinner at Joe's Stone Crab in Miami and solved the problems of the world. Well, not really, but with his help, she'd seen her way forward, seen journalism as her shining path.

She'd waxed philosophical, over a second glass of Chardonnay, expounding that the writing had to contain both the warp and weft of society in order to help readers make sense of it. He'd warned that one man's good was another's bad. "It's not bad versus good," she'd countered. "It was two interpretations, and both were needed."

Over the years, she'd seen that reporting usually weighed heavier on the "woe" side of life; that news tended to be bad news, and that writers had to dig hard and argue loud to place a story of *good* news. She saw, though, that it was the balance, the reassurance, the sense of hope that helped people make it through the disasters, be they global, national, regional or personal.

She'd come to embrace the word "weal"—which at one point had been "commonweal," as though the state of oneself and the state of one's community were interconnected. It made sense of the "pursuit of happiness" at the core of the American dream, so anyone who touched even the hem of that garment deserved to be "news."

"To write the warp and weft, the woe and weal." Those first thoughts had evolved, until she'd created her parallelogram of a boiled-down mission statement. She'd included it into her scholarship documents, as guidance for recipients.

She glanced over to where her notebook computer rested on the little desk near the window. Next to it, her small portable printer had spewed forth the pages she'd completed so far. She didn't know, yet, exactly what she was writing. A memoir? A plan for the future? It could be a legacy document for journalists, something those future scholarship recipients would receive along with their stipend. Or it might be a journal no one would ever read. Whatever it turned out to be, she knew it had personal significance.

She'd worried, lately, about the scope of her career. Had she written with enough substance? Delved deeply enough into the subject matters she'd covered? Had she held bad actors to account, uncovered corruption where she could, and upheld heroes where she'd found them?

She mentally reviewed some of the case files she really had archived in details, those "deadline" files about NASA, the Arctic, Pelagic flora and fauna, Tokyo, Hong Kong, and several others.

Chris had also discovered a core belief that'd probably been buried too deep for her to distinguish until recently. As it turned out, she believed she occupied a particular nook in the universe that only she could fulfill. She believed everyone did.

She realized, now, that part of the truth-telling at the heart of her work was her capacity to see the quiddity of a person, project, or thing—the quality that makes that thing what it is. And yet, she hadn't been turning that lens on herself.

She'd read about purpose, calling, and even destiny in recent years. She'd found her favorite quotation on the subject in the writings of Mary Baker Eddy: "Each individual must fill his own niche in time and eternity." That said it about perfectly.

What seemed oddly irrelevant in her current writing was time, normally such an important carrier of internal waymarks. Its normal passage had been eluding her lately. Mostly, she'd let it go as she recovered from that nasty knock on the head, dismissing the problem as short-term memory loss resulting from the injury.

But her head no longer hurt, the bump had disappeared, and time still wasn't marching along in any way she could call normal. She lost track of it constantly. When she expected to wake up in the morning, it might be the middle of the night. When she thought it was winter, she'd find herself in a different season.

This, she knew, was what had her feeling so restless. Some piece of the puzzle was missing, and she had the sense she could find it if she listened for some inner guidance, another practice that was somewhat new to her, but increasingly important.

She stood and stretched, peering out the window of the second-story room that offered a view northward up the coast. In the distance she could see the faint blinking of the Piedras light competing with the still-bright sky. *I think I need a walk. Maybe along the bluff?*

As she walked, perhaps she'd be pondering further what her ultimate purpose might be. Mark Twain famously said "The two most important days in your life are the day you are born and the day you find out why."

Chris arrived at the dead end where the lovely bluff trail began. Someday it would connect to the California Coastal Trail that many coastal communities were working on. When completed —probably decades hence—it would extend from the Oregon coast to Mexico. For now, local committees worked on it segment by segment. Just south of her in Cambria, the trail was coming along nicely, as it was here in Milford-Haven, with ongoing volunteer teams in place for maintenance and educational programs.

Chris stepped out of her SUV and a gust of wind nearly whipped the door out of her hand. *Wow, that came suddenly,* she thought, reaching inside for her hat and scarf. She locked the car, pocketed the keys and entered at the northern trail head, noticing the scent of lavender, though she didn't see any of the flowers in bloom. Though she'd hiked portions of this trail before, she didn't remember it being nearly so well developed.

Autumn lay across the Central Coast gently. Tall grasses and wheat tufts joined a medley of tans and browns, russets and burnt oranges, creating one of the most stunning palettes of the year—far more subtle than the vivid pops of color in spring, but lovely in its own way.

Still can't believe it's autumn, when I thought it was Winter Solstice at the lighthouse. I keep getting things out of sequence.

Determined to enjoy the beautiful day, and get whatever she'd come to the trail to find, she inhaled the tang of sea air and considered the subtle tonalities that surrounded her. In Japan they called it *shibui*, as she'd learned when living there for a couple of years early in her career. Thinking about the neutral tones she'd used to decorate her condo in Santa Maria, she thought again what a strong influence Japan had on her, at least in terms of design. She aspired to their sophisticated simplicity, which seemed a contradiction in terms but was in fact a perfect synchrony.

A beautiful carved wooden bench provided a comfortable overlook of the view. Though a woman sat at one end, Chris knew this was a public park, and approached. "Hope you don't mind."

Chris sat, then looked more closely at her companion. *Oh my, it's a scarecrow! So life like!* Chris turned her gaze to the ocean, inhaled the fresh sea breeze, and watched as a necklace of pelicans trailed low across the horizon.

"I don't mind," a woman's voice said.

"Ack!" Chris nearly jumped up. "Oh! I . . . I thought you were. . . ."

The woman turned her head to meet her gaze.

"Sorry! You sat so still. . . . On Main Street I saw some scarecrows. I thought you were one."

"Ha ha ha ha ha." The woman's response burst out, a staccato series of monosyllables. "I've been called worse."

Chris gave her own short burst of a laugh. "I apologize."

The woman held an edition of *The Milford-Haven News*, and she offered it to Chris, who glanced down to see a headline about the local Scarecrow Festival. Chris picked up the paper and read further. The Festival had launched recently in the neighboring town of Cambria. She skimmed over words describing their mission to provide a sustainable, inclusive, collaborative set of programs to encourage artistic creativity and visibility.

"What a nice idea," Chris said, handing back the pages, which flapped in the breeze. "Hope it's a great success."

"It will be," said the woman confidently. The two sat together in companionable silence for a while, until the woman asked, "Notice the date?"

"Uh, no," Chris admitted. When the woman held the front page up for her to inspect again, Chris inhaled sharply. "October 31 . . . 2009? But . . . it's a misprint. I mean, this is 1996!"

"Well, that's the thing."

Chris could feel her heart thumping heavily in her chest. "What thing?"

"Time. It's not exactly real, you know?"

Why is she talking about time? The very thing that's been worrying me . . . the reason I came on this hike. She tried to settle her pulse. *Who is this woman? Maybe she's a homeless person who was let out of an institution. Maybe she's a psychopath.* Chris glanced behind, and looked at the trail leading away in both directions. *No one else in sight.* "Uh, that's an interesting theory."

"Not exactly theoretical, depending upon whom you believe. Quantum mechanics says the flow of time is universal and absolute. But Einstein's Theory of General Relativity says the flow of time is, of course, relative. Malleable. Fluid.

She may be nuts, but she's smart. Beginning to feel intrigued enough that her flight-response stopped being triggered, Chris said, "So I've read."

"I think, in the end, we have it both ways."

"Hmm. You mean, absolute by day, fluid by night, when we dream?"

"Something like that. But who says all dreams happen at night?"

"Oh, are you talking about lucid dreaming?"

"That comes close."

"It's a fascinating subject. I did some research on it for a story. I, uh, do features."

"For television, yes. I've seen some of your work."

"Oh. I—" Chris felt embarrassed as she often did when she encountered a viewer in public.

"They're quite good. The one on child adoption was exceptional."

Chris felt herself blush. "I . . . thank you." *Wish I could ask her why it touched her. Was she adopted? Was someone in her family?*

The woman continued. "The lucid dreaming report included some of the twentieth century studies, but it started long before."

Chris turned her head sharply. "I know. My producer told me not to try to video a doctoral thesis."

"Ha ha ha ha ha." The woman's stacatto laugh escaped again, then drifted away on the wind.

"Well, that struck your funny bone, and you're very well informed. Are you a professor?"

"Not a professor, but a teacher, yes."

When the student is ready, the teacher will appear. The old aphorism pronounced itself in Chris's mind almost as clearly as if it'd been spoken aloud.

"That's exactly right, you know. The teacher *does* appear."

The hackles stood straight up on Chris's neck and her body jumped in startlement, sending her a few inches farther down the bench."What the. . . . Who the. . . ."

"Let me ask *you* a question," the woman said calmly. "What would you say if the newspaper's date is not a misprint?"

A swirl of fog rose up across the water from where they sat, pearlescent and beautiful, like the inside of a sea shell. Yet something about it reminded her of the sudden storm that'd lately menaced her at the lighthouse. Keeping the cloud in her peripheral vision, Chris asked, "What on earth does that mean?"

The woman said, "We were discussing the fluidity of time, and lucid dreaming. Does something about this experience feel like a dream?"

Chris's heart began again to beat heavily. "I . . . what if it does?"

"Well, it's an opportunity to pay attention, ask questions, investigate. Something you're good at. Something you love to do."

Chris took a deep breath. "That's true. Okay. So you're saying I could, at this very moment, be experiencing a lucid dream. In broad daylight."

"Why not?" the woman asked. "If you're experiencing time in fluid form, then there's no reason why we couldn't be looking at a newspaper article published in 2009."

"In a dream," Chris emphasized.

"For a while, we do go back and forth: into the relatively perceivable form, the agreed upon chronology. We live a life time, with glimpses of the fluid form."

Chris looked out across the water, where the pearlescent cloud expanded, twisting itself into a spiral that climbed high into the heavens. Was it the numinous phenomenon it appeared to be? Or was it a figment of the waking dream in which she now found herself? Chris began to shake. "I'm sorry, I'm feeling cold, and I—"

"It's time, Christine."

"I never told you my name. Did you follow me here? Who the hell are you?"

"I arrived here before you did, you might recall." The woman turned toward Chris, and her face seemed to luminesce with an expression of more kindness than anything Chris had ever seen.

"There's absolutely nothing to fear. You're in a lucid dream. And from this perspective, it's possible to understand so much more."

"So I . . . I'm not really here?" Chris heard the tremble in her own voice.

"Of course you are, dear. You're really here. Just in a new way."

"That woman at the lighthouse . . . those people at the circle of stones . . ."

"We've all been trying to show you," the woman said gently.

Chris began to feel tears pool in her eyes. She looked down at the newspaper rattling in the wind. "I didn't make it, did I? That's why it's all been so . . . so bizarre. That's why Del . . . he's investigating . . . " She jabbed a finger at the masthead date. "Will I be here *then?*"

"Time isn't so important any more, is it? You're here now."

"Del! He's investigating in 1996! I've been missing because . . . but . . . he can see me! He can hear me!"

"He has the Sight, yes. When he dreams."

"Lucid dreaming. So that's . . . that's the key. How I can still be heard. But I'm not really . . . not really here."

The woman placed a hand on Chris's arm. "You're here whenever you need to be, for as long as they need you, and you need them."

Chris pondered this for a moment. "You mean . . . it's up to me?"

"Nothing happens without your consent," the woman said, a strange echo in her voice.

Chris looked again at the cloud. "So that means I can help him solve the case," she said with determination. As it always did when she sensed she was getting to the truth of a story, her mind began fitting together the pieces of the puzzle she now saw more clearly even as new questions formed. She turned to her companion to start asking them. But the bench was empty.

Chris raced back down the trail as if her hair were on fire, leapt into her car and made it back to her motel room. In a dead panic, she bent over and tried to steady her breathing.

Dead panic. That's funny!

As her nerves began to steady, she felt swamped with sadness and disappointment. *It was all for nothing. She glanced at the pages she'd written. And that's all for nothing, too. Does it even exist in the real world? I can't tell what's real!*

She sat on the edge of the bed and wept. Then she rolled over into a fetal position and wept harder. *Why am I here? Why do I feel solid, real? What's the point?*

After a while, the crying subsided and her breath came in gasps. The desperation began to ebb and her thoughts began to clear, her reporter skills coming to the fore.

I died. Might as well admit that much. But I'm still here. I have to admit that, too. So that answers one major question! A half-laugh burst from her throat.

All this while, her head hadn't wanted to admit it. And her heart had ignored every warning and every sign. But her soul had suspected the truth.

So this journey, the life journey, it's real. And it continues. What had the woman said? That I'd be here as long as I need them, and they need me.

If she approached this story as she would any other, she'd ask the key questions. *What?* A journalist following a lead. *Where?* Last known destination connected to that lead, the Clarke house. *Why?* To meet with a contact to get an important piece of information for this story. *When?* She couldn't begin to answer that one, but her journals would show the date of the Clarke house meet. Finally, *Who?* That was the big question.

Del had been right when they'd first met in his conference room while he watched her videos. He'd asked whether she'd had "help" falling into that hole.

Her eyes widened and her breath caught again in her trachea. *I did have help! I was pushed! I was . . . killed!* And now, finally, a new and overdue emotion surfaced: anger. Someone had shoved her aside, probably for money. She dredged the memory of his face from the depths of the despair where she'd buried it. *That's right. He didn't bury me. I buried him!*

Her skilled powers of observation focused and she saw him as clearly as if a powerful beam of light unmasked him where he stood in that unfinished house. He had dared to harm her, to presume he could alter her destiny, throw her off course. Well, she was now on course again, and would never be thrown off it again.

That murderer had thought he'd gotten away with his crime. But now she knew he wouldn't, not only because she was a witness, but because she had someone who could and would prove what had happened. Detective Delmar.

Del can hear me. He can see me. He's been pursuing my case. Now she knew she'd have to stay here, stay close to Del until he had the proof he needed. *He has to find out exactly what happened.*

And that's not all. He'd have to find the motive for the murder, who was behind it, why they had wanted to stop her, and what they were trying to conceal.

To the silent room, Chris spoke aloud. "I can help Del. And that's exactly what I'll do."

Chapter 21

Delmar had stopped by the home of artist Miranda Jones, following up on her call about a possible intruder.

Visiting with Miranda was always a treat. A kind and lovely young woman, she often engaged in some project to contribute to the community. What he really liked, though, was the spark that always seemed to animate her. *Her creativity. That must be what keeps that fire lit.*

She'd been ready for his visit with a pot of tea brewing, and she'd invited him to sit at her long oak table. Before sitting, he asked where exactly she'd heard the noise that'd bothered her and her cat—the sleek black beauty that now lay curled at the end of the sofa.

Miranda pointed to the deck, and he'd slid open the slider, closing it behind him. Before moving away from the door, he took a close look at the planks where he did see a couple of dusty prints that might've been made by shoes, but these could have been the owners. Next, he peered over the railing down to the duff, but again saw nothing conclusive.

When he stepped around the corner where the deck wrapped toward the French doors into her studio, he practically skidded to a stop when his nostrils were assaulted by the strong aroma of lavender. He looked again at the forest floor below, and checked for potted plants that might hold the distinctive purple flower, but saw none.

Del took a deep breath. *Chris was here. Maybe she still is.* Why had she come to Miranda's studio? To draw him here? But she had other, more effective ways of reaching him. He'd have to solve that later.

For now, he knew the identity of Miranda's visitor, and found it interesting that the cat had sensed her, too—just as Kuyama's dog had done. But he couldn't share this information with Miranda.

"I saw no evidence of trespass," Del said when they sat at her table.

"Well, then I guess it was a benign spirit."

Del looked at her sharply.

"Today is May 3rd, right?"

He nodded.

" I mean, it is National Paranormal Day, after all."

The two acquaintances laughed out loud. The humor covered the relief he felt at not having to explain the ephemeral guest that'd stopped by.

Del headed home, once the rest of his daily rounds were completed.

He followed his usual routine, changing clothes, heating up a frozen dinner and, after washing his dishes, settling at his kitchen table to review current cases.

From his briefcase, he pulled out a stack of work, which always included the Chris Christian file these days. But when he fingered through the tabbed folders he saw two he was sure he hadn't seen before.

Don't tell me this is gonna be like finding more lighthouse stamps in her notebook! Though he'd accepted that as a special element of their inexplicable communication, he kept hoping he could keep three out of four limbs in the real world as he pursued her case.

When they'd met at Kuyama's, she'd said she had files for him in her car. Of course, he'd never actually seen them and had dismissed the possibility he ever would, unless he found them during some future search of her premises, should he ever gain access again.

But one of these files was labeled "Chernak" and the sight of it raised his hackles. *She mentioned this guy, the husband of Stacey Chernak, the woman I met in Morro Bay.* Another tab read "Clarke Shipping/ Clarke House." *Her last known location.* And a third, neatly printed in her handwriting, read "Mole Guy." *Who in the world is that?* The fourth new file was labeled "Legacy," and it brought a sudden, poignant sense of sadness.

Del sat still for a moment, realizing he likely now had new leads to follow. But how had he received them? And how could he explain to the brass—or to anyone—how he'd come by the information he expected to find in these files?

Exhaling, he separated these new files from the rest of the pile, intending to set them aside for now. But on the first file a sticky note was affixed, also printed in her hand:

For Delmar, if I don't make it back.

His throat tightened as he fought down the grief. The last time they'd met, she'd had no apparent awareness of her own transition state, no sense that she'd lost her life, though it seemed clear she was struggling to find a new one—or a viable new form by means of which to continue her journey.

But did this note mean she knew, now, what had happened to her?

The aroma of lavender swirled through the kitchen. When he dreamt tonight, would he be having his next meeting with Chris? If so, he'd best be ready.

Epilogue

May 31, 1997
Milford-Haven, California
by Emily Wilkins, Staff Reporter, *Milford-Haven News*

Christine Christian, a well-known television journalist, has now been designated officially as a Missing Person by the SLO County Sheriff's Department.

Deputy Delmar Johnson, who had been reviewing her disappearance as a Cold Case over the last several months, said new evidence indicates she may have been abducted or murdered.

Since Ms. Christian traveled frequently for her work, both nationally and internationally, and had met all pending deadlines at the time, it was thought that her absence was related either to an assignment or an extended vacation.

More recently, however, she failed to submit a scheduled video program. It is the first time in her career the multiple-award-winning journalist had failed to meet a deadline.

Return soon to . . .
Milford-Haven!
Available now . . .

Mara Purl's
What the Heart Knows

Novel One
in the exciting Milford-Haven saga

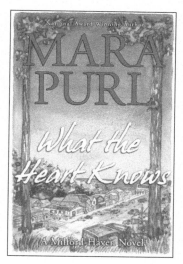

Enjoy the following Preview
from the novel . . .

Prologue

Broadcast journalist Christine Christian stepped down from her black car into an even blacker night.

She extended her leg past the running board of the Ford Explorer, waiting till her shoe found the hardened dirt of the rutted road. *Actually, I'm inside the gates, so this'll be the driveway,* she thought, barely able to see the ground since dousing her headlights.

Cool sea wind tumbled through the air, carrying with it the fresh tang of kelp. Her hair ruffling, she glanced overhead to look for the moon. *I know it's nearly full, and it rose early tonight.* But the sky appeared moonless, and such stars as normally sparkled in the clear, windswept autumn air were obscured by dense cloud cover.

A hundred feet below the bluff, the sea pounded. An October storm had been traveling the South Pacific, and even this far north, the Central Coast reverberated with the effects. "Generating winds of up to fifty miles per hour . . . " she remembered her KOST-SATV colleague saying on this evening's broadcast.

On her left, the terrain fell away to the ocean—now nothing more than an inky, undulating mass. To the northwest, the flash of the Piedras Blancas lighthouse winked in the darkness, sweeping across the landscape to reveal a ghostly skeleton of the unfinished mansion.

Even by its outline, she could tell this Clarke House held something special in its design. Having studied the architectural drawings, she found the reality of the physical structure intriguing. Though she'd read that some of the locals objected to its massive size being ostentatious and out of place, she could see it also fit the site as though it belonged. *The way skyscrapers fit Manhattan.*

The image of a cityscape seemed incongruous, and she stood still a moment longer, waiting for it to make sense. *Funny, when I was a kid growing up in this little town, all I wanted to do was get away—get to a big city. And I did. But now I find myself drawn back here.* Yes, that was it . . . processing the fact that, after her many travels, she should find herself once again in Milford-Haven.

For one thing, there was the job with KOST in Santa Maria. After several years on-camera for the broadcast networks— mostly NBC—she'd made the switch to satellite. With the 1996 Telecommunications Act, Congress had signaled its intention to create a pro-competitive deregulatory policy—a turning point for the TV business. She'd ridden that new wave, taking the title of Special Correspondent, which meant decent pay and great freedom to develop her own content. Her three-part piece on adoption had just been shown in the Central Coast region. *Part three aired Sunday—two days ago.*

She was already gathering material for her next three-parter on earthquakes, a story that would be taking her to San Francisco, then to Japan and to Turkey. *My bags are all packed. I'm spending three days in San Fran researching the '89 Loma Prieta quake. Then I leave for Tokyo from there.*

Now, there was this story that had brought her to Milford-Haven. *What a strange homecoming. I should come back in the daylight, visit the newspaper where I had my first job . . . see what's the best little spot for breakfast these days . . . walk on Touchstone Beach. If my wandering soul has a home, it's probably here.*

Chris took a step away from the bluff, aware once again of the dark that surrounded her. *What am I doing here now? Pursuing a lead, as usual.* She sighed. *Better get this over with. Wish I'd worn sturdier shoes than these flats.* Chilled in the wind, she pulled her jacket closer and drew on the pair of leather gloves she'd tucked in her pocket.

Adjusting the long diagonal strap of the compact purse she wore slung across her body, she hefted her flashlight and clicked it on. She picked her way over construction debris and uneven terrain toward the front of the house, where eventually stairs would lead up to the entrance. Stepping onto a narrow plank that trembled under her feet, she dashed upward, then leapt off to stand just inside the foyer. *Ack! I thought it was dark outside—but inside it's pitch black.*

Chris stood still, trying to focus. Minutes passed, yet her pulse wouldn't settle. Shifting her feet, she tried to find a piece of floor unlittered with . . . what? Nails, concrete clumps, snips of wire? Still she waited, hoping her eyes would make a further adjustment to the unrelieved darkness.

The house seemed to sway with the wind and crashing surf, unsteady on its underpinnings. *That's an illusion, I'm sure. It's my own legs that're unsteady. Dammit it, Chris! You know what they say about Curiosity.*

She stood in what would undoubtedly be the living room — an expanse framed by a crosswork of beams, exposed for now, with a space left open on one whole side for a future wall of glass. *I was right. The lines are good, and the view will be spectacular.*

On the opposite wall, flagstone had already been fashioned into an oversized fireplace. It seemed curiously complete in this incomplete room—except for the rectangular hole with the ends of a ladder just visible.

The plans showed a hearthstone goes there—imported marble. She'd noticed this detail had shown up on both sets of plans. *Remember, one detail can make the story.* Reed had always told her that, and he was the best reporter in the business. *He did get in trouble once, though, covering that story in Ohio. Safe home after reporting in Vietnam, and then he's almost killed in that deserted house. He told me later he had the feeling he shouldn't go there.*

A chill swept over her now, and the fine hairs on the back of her neck tingled. *What's my intuition saying? I should leave this place.* This swaying, unhallowed structure menaced with its protruding metal splinters and ragged concrete edges.

But what was this so-called intuition that she shouldn't have come here? Wasn't that just fear? After all, she'd been led to this location—vectored here by one clue after another. *I can either be a wimp, or a good reporter. Logic says there's something to be discovered. I have to find out what.*

The first clue had been little more than an inkling . . . *or more like a rankling,* she recalled. Learning a mansion was being built in Milford-Haven—a first for the cozy artist-town —she'd called Sawyer Construction for an interview. Foremost among her list of questions was whether or not the likelihood of a new earthquake code would present fresh challenges either to design or to construction.

Geography, geology, seismology . . . these were three of Chris's pet subjects. Ever since the 1994 Northridge earthquake, she'd been tracking not only press coverage, but also published scientific papers about the possibility of new building codes. That quake had included what the seismologists called "unexpected moment frame damages." FEMA was now looking carefully at steel strength and possible detrimental effects on connection design.

Before conducting any interview, Chris always did careful research to be better prepared with good questions. *But,* she admitted, *I also do it to butter-up my subject.* The odd thing was that Jack Sawyer—rather than being flattered by the attention of a reporter who could speak at least some of his own language —had seemed by turns diffident and defensive and, ultimately, disingenuous. *A man with something to hide?*

A sound—a snap of fabric?—yanked her from her thoughts and sent her heartrate skyrocketing. She held her breath and heard the sound again. Like an exhalation, plastic wrapped over vacant window openings was sucked and pulled against the tape holding it to the framework. *Just the wind.* Perhaps the house itself was breathing, trying to expel its bad humors.

Chris took a step onto something that rolled under her foot, throwing her off balance. She caught herself by bracing against a low cinderblock wall, tearing a piece of skin from her palm. She yelped in the dark, but at least the jab of pain had served to sharpen her attention.

The reasons she'd come here began to return to her mind in an orderly progression. First, there'd been the call from an anonymous tipster that there might be something strange about the plans for the Clarke House. She'd confirmed this with her own investigation, discovering the house had *two* sets of plans. She'd needed an explanation, but hadn't wanted to tip her hand to Sawyer too soon.

Then my source called me again. He was right about the plans. Chances are he's right in everything he says about this house. He was an elusive informant—a phone contact she thought of as "Mr. Man," since he refused to give his name, who called with tantalizing fragments of information. She tried to fit them together like so many shards of broken crystal, clear and sharp-edged.

He'd said to meet him here, so here she was trying to gather more fragments of this story, and she found herself resenting it. *Joseph will be waiting at Calma with a clandestine dinner for two. Tonight's our make-up date after our little tiff. He planned a midnight supper . . . all the more romantic for the secrecy, the hour . . . and the rapprochement.*

The thought hastened her, and she tried again to focus on the incomplete room. Lifting her flashlight, she began inspecting the spaces framed by raw beams. She stepped through an opening. *This will be the kitchen.* She could see where the crew had marked identifiable icons for drains and faucets, lines to indicate cabinets and pantry. *All of this seems normal enough. Where's the story? I wonder what Mr. Man wants to show me?*

One thing that'd varied between the two sets of plans was something about the steel: different manufacturers, but also different grades. She figured a quick look at exposed steel beams under the house would reveal which steel had actually been used.

How do I get down there? She walked from the kitchen across the expanse of the living room and discovered a stairwell against the far wall. But at the moment it contained neither stairs nor a plank. She thought back for a moment. *Oh . . . there was a ladder in that opening by the fireplace.* Cursing again, she began walking carefully toward the gaping hole.

Just then another sound reached her—closer than the persistent wind and crashing surf. *What was that? A scrape . . . a footfall? Or is that Mr. Man? About time he got here. But I didn't see any headlights. What if it's not him?* Clicking off her flashlight, she pressed her body against the closest beam. *I'm alone in a wind-swept rattletrap of wood beams and metal scraps, and I should've been home doing my nails before driving to Santa Barbara to meet Joseph.*

She breathed deeply and tried to picture herself arriving home, refreshing her polish and makeup, locking the door behind her, starting the SUV's engine. *Details.* They were always her best defense against fear.

She listened a moment longer, hearing no further scraping. *Just my nerves.* She clicked her flashlight back on, then continued toward the hearth-well. The ladder itself seemed to disappear into the depths. "It's the blackest hole I've ever seen," she muttered. "Blacker than a black cat's ass—on black velvet."

"There's a quick way down there, Ms. Christian."

"Ahh!" She whirled toward the voice that'd burst out of nowhere. "Who—?" *That's not my contact's voice.* Her throat spasmed, and she gulped air, her heart pounding louder than the surf. "Where—?" She gasped. "You just about scared the. . . ." Struggling for calm, she clutched her flashlight and tried to keep its beam from bouncing across the man's features.

His seamed face loomed over a hulking physique. *Any distinguishing marks? Yes! I thought it was a shadow, but that's a mole on his left cheek . . . size of a quarter. Can't really see his eyes.* She inhaled. "What . . . what are you doing here?"

"The question should be what are *you* doing here, Ms. Christian. *I* work here." The voice was steady, self-assured.

"Of course you do." *Why does he know my name?* She struggled for a casual tone. "Good thing you're here, because I could really use some help." A laugh erupted from her throat like a burst of static from a malfunctioning radio. "Actually, I wanted to look around in the basement, but it's so hard to see in the dark."

The guy said nothing. Chris wondered how long she could keep producing an uninterrupted stream of words, hoping to use them like a protective force field. Keep talking. *Redirect the focus to him.* "Say, you didn't even bring a flashlight."

"Very observant."

Get a conversation going. "Guess we both counted on moonlight."

"Not with these clouds."

"You must know the house real well if you work here." *Burly muscles, heavy work boots.* "One of the construction crew, huh?"

"Right again."

"Well, listen, I'm running late for an appointment and someone's waiting for me. He tends to get upset when I'm not on time. I'll come back in the daylight when I can see better." She made a move away from the hearth-well, but it only brought her closer to him. As she took another step, her foot caught on something, pitching her forward.

The worker's arm shot out in front of her, his large hand capturing hers as she regained her balance. *He couldn't stop the impulse to catch me.* She stood toe-to-toe with him now, and could smell alcohol on his breath as he exhaled. *Probably a bourbon drinker,* she noted, unable to stop cataloguing details.

His hand opened suddenly. She slipped hers free and stepped back. *Has his brief moment of gallantry put him enough off balance that I can appeal to him? Don't I always reach people with my authenticity and with my words?* She looked up into the weathered face, trying to make eye contact, but could see nothing more than a glint. "Thanks so much for taking care of me."

He paused, then smiled. "Oh, I haven't taken care of you yet."

Damn! "But you're about to, am I right?"

A chuckle rumbled in his barrel chest. "Too right."

Good! Maybe I did reach him this time . . . I made him laugh. How many times have I talked my way out of a tight spot? How many times have I played out this kind of scenario in my head?

Time seemed to slow, and her perspective shifted until she watched the stand-off between herself and burly-guy from a slight distance, as though she were discussing the angle with her television camera crew. *It's an over-the-shoulder two-shot, like one of my interviews. Then we cut to a close-up that shows the mole, the craggy face—trying to give the audience a chance to read his expression.*

Now her view altered and the setting was a Western: a black-hatted hulk blocked the path of a red-dressed spit-fire. *Whose story is this? When did it happen? Why are we in the Old West?* She almost seemed to recognize the scene . . . from a story by her favorite writer, Louis L'Amour. *Never let the opponent gain the advantage, his narration advised. Don't wait. Make the first move.*

The scene shifted again, and now she saw herself as Emma Peel in *The Avengers.* Skilled in martial arts, undaunted by her precarious predicament, the heroine faces her adversary. *Emma kicks out with those long legs, takes her man by surprise.*

Suddenly, Chris found herself standing in her own shoes, opposite her own bad guy. He might be bigger, stronger, more massive, but maneuverability was on *her* side. *It's now or never!*

She clicked off her flashlight and hurled it at his head. She'd already chosen exactly what direction she would run—past him, not away, because that would be unexpected. In the sudden blackness she knew she'd have a second's worth of advantage. It was just the second she needed.

She leapt forward, and saw his fist too late. It impacted her temple with the force of an explosion, hurtling her backward into the gaping hearth-well. Her body seemed to hang for a moment, suspended in space—until it smashed against the dirt, forcing the last molecule of air from her lungs. *I can't breathe. I can't move.*

Her eyes blinked in the dark, her mind searched for options. She saw his huge feet land on the dirt near her, and kept her eyes still. *If he thinks I'm already dead he'll just leave me. Don't breathe!*

He was carrying something . . . a shovel. No! He stepped on its edge, forcing it into the big pile of soft earth, lifting a load of it, moving it toward her head.

Just before the dirt hit her face, she closed her eyes. *I'm covered enough now that he can't see me. I'll breathe soon.*

Another shovelful landed on her chest, its weight sodden. Now another was flung over her face.

It'd been too many seconds since air had found its way into her lungs, and with a sudden clarity, she realized she had never taken that breath.

Desperately, she inhaled, but she found no oxygen. Only the wet, sandy home-soil of the Central Coast.

Return soon to . . .
Milford-Haven!
Available now . . .

Mara Purl's
Where the Heart Lives

Novel Two
in the exciting Milford-Haven saga

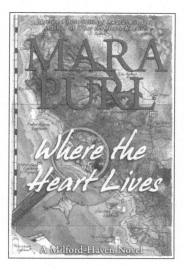

Enjoy the following Preview
from the novel . . .

Prologue

Senior Deputy Delmar Johnson, startled at a tapping sound, darted a look around his shadowed office.

Just the rain . . . or the wind. There it was again. Like some-one's knocking to get in. His scalp prickling, he pushed back from his desk. Remaining seated, he interlaced his long fingers and reached overhead to stretch his back.

Still, he couldn't shake his feeling of foreboding. Highway 1 stretched past his window, a slick ribbon of asphalt devoid of traffic. He'd stayed in his office long enough that now it was dark outside. Daylight hours had grown short, and December rains doused the Central Coast much of the day—again.

Television journalist Christine Christian was still listed as a missing person. *Hate to think of anyone stuck out in this weather . . . living . . . or dead. Plenty of people in the "Missing" files. Seven weeks, now, and no one seems to know what's happened to the popular broadcaster.*

According to the satellite station where she had a contract, Christian had planned to drive north to the Bay Area to do seismic research for a few days. Then she'd been scheduled to fly to Tokyo from the local airport. *That makes sense . . . study earthquakes in San Francisco, and in Japan.* She'd never made her flight, however, and never turned up anywhere else.

When her boss reported her missing, the sheriff's department had checked her Santa Maria condo, but found nothing amiss, and her rent paid for months in advance. Her car wasn't at her residence and hadn't been discovered at the airport.

Though there were no real leads, Del did have a police sketch of an unnamed man who'd visited Sally's Restaurant in Milford-Haven. Owner Sally O'Mally herself had seen and talked to this guy, who'd said at the time he was looking for the journalist. But circulation of both that sketch and Christine's photograph, had yielded nothing further, at which point the case had been filed away. Officially, Del had let it go. Yet something about the case wouldn't let go of him.

Why does a successful journalist—on her way to what sounds like an exciting trip—suddenly fall off the radar? According to the DMV, she owned a black Ford Explorer. *If, instead of taking the more usual 101, she drove Highway 1 . . . all those treacherous curves along the coast . . . that black car of hers could be hidden at the bottom of some steep ravine or even submerged in a rocky cove. Might take us months to locate it.*

On the other hand, she wouldn't be the first person who'd decided to slip away from a job—or from a relationship.

There'd been nothing new for weeks. But now the cold case could be warming up. Today's call wasn't a break exactly, but at least it could be a starting point.

Mr. Joseph Calvin—a wealthy icon of Santa Barbara society— had reported a connection with the journalist, but had asked that Captain Sandoval oversee the matter personally.

Sandoval had assigned Detective Dexter. *And for some reason, Dex wants me in on the interview with him. And he said not to be in uniform.* Apparently, Calvin had called to explain that—though he didn't feel he had any actual information relevant to Ms. Christian's disappearance—he did know her, and thought it likely he'd seen her close to the time she must've gone missing. He'd added that he'd like to keep his cooperation as discreet as possible. Otherwise, the press would probably have their typical field day, which would not only be unpleasant for him, but might also harm their investigation.

Dex had placed the call and discovered that the earliest time Mr. Calvin could be available was this evening. Though he'd be at a charity function, he'd cut it short and return to his residence for a ten p.m. meeting with Dexter and Johnson.

Time to hit the road. Del wondered what it'd be like for a bastion of white society to be questioned in his home late at night, especially with one white officer, and one black. *You never know how someone will feel about race until you get past the first veneer of manners.*

Del pulled on his all-weather jacket and headed outside. Making sure the building was locked, he pressed his vehicle's keyless entry remote, its mechanical chirp still an uncommon sound on the Central Coast. One of the perks of being a member of the Special Problems Unit was access to four-by-four vehicles. The Suburban coughed into activity and, a few moments later, settled into a deep, growling purr as it gathered speed.

For the moment, this stretch of Highway 1 appeared safe and clear. But the mean streets of his own childhood in South Central L.A. sometimes rose out of the dark to haunt him. If a car backfired, he always first assumed it was a gunshot, his body reflexively tensing, his senses coming to full alert. Even after twenty-six months on the Central Coast, he hadn't yet unlearned those inner-city reactions. *Perhaps*, he thought as the Suburban ate up the miles, *I never will. Indeed, perhaps I never should.*

Though he still had much to learn about his new area, he'd been spending some of his free time browsing local libraries. The San Luis Obispo County Library system turned out to have several branches along the north-south route Del routinely traveled, each with its own distinct character. The hub was in SLO—thanks to a 1903 grant from Andrew Carnegie that established the first library in the county. He enjoyed the branches in Morro Bay and Cambria, but his favorite was Milford-Haven's odd little library tucked away on a side street. Despite the historic-looking brick facade, renovations to the interior seemed relatively new. *Have to investigate sometime.*

His reading varied widely from studies of the local architecture and landscaping to its political history, surprisingly rich in multicultural lore that held a particular appeal for Del. And though Santa Barbara now occupied its own county to the south, the indigenous people who'd lived here first had seen it as one land, nestled against the coastal range. Through the centuries, it seemed new arrivals were always eager to confis-cate its assets and claim its spectacular terrain for their own: first the Spanish; then the Mexicans; ultimately, the Americans.

Where I'm heading tonight was in the thick of it at one time. Interesting that's where my meeting is. The story he'd read had resonated powerfully: betrayal and dislocation, if not actual slavery. In the 1880s, the Indian Agent Thomas Hope was put in charge of protecting the Chumash who lived high on the mountains overlooking the ocean in their Kashwa Reservation. Instead, he evicted them. *Today it's known as the Hope Ranch.*

Del rolled his shoulders and blew out an exhalation. He'd kept his radio on low volume. Now, halfway to his destination, he heard, "Twenty-four-Z-four."

"Zebra-four," he answered quickly. He'd been the last to join the four-person SPU, and that had given him the number "four."

"Ten-twenty-one as soon as possible."

"Ten-four."

Ten-twenty-one meant "call base" on a closed line and twenty-four was the number for the main station at San Luis. Del used his cell phone to dial the number. *Who needs to talk with me privately without using the radio?*

"Dispatch," the sheriff's office answered.

"This is Delmar Johnson."

"I'll put you through."

The night sped by outside the Suburban, and Del watched the road. Zebra was the code name for the SPU. Well, the old adage says *"When you hear hoofbeats, think horses, not zebras."* He chuckled to himself. *That works for the usual cases. But we catch the special problems.* He got serious as his superior came back on the line.

"Dex here. Sorry to give you such short notice, but you'll have to handle the Calvin interview on your own."

"Oh?"

"I know, irregular procedure, but we're short-handed tonight, and I'm still tied up at a situation over on the I-5. No way I can get to Santa Barbara in time."

"Should I cancel? Explain to Mr. Calvin that we could see him tomorrow?"

"No. I don't know what's so urgent, but the word came down from Sandoval that we should speak to Calvin tonight. The man'll probably be impressed by a suit ringing his doorbell so quickly after he volunteered to meet with us."

Del glanced at his sleeve. *Damn. Not wearing a suit.* "Anything in particular I should ask him?"

"No, you know what to do. Standard stuff. You have good instincts. Fill me in first thing tomorrow."

"Will do." Del closed his cell phone and kept his foot steady on the accelerator. Mr. Calvin was in for a little surprise this evening. *One officer, not two—the black one—and in casual clothes, as though I'm dropping by for a chat.*

Del was eager to gauge his response. *You can tell a lot about a guy by his first reaction to the unexpected.*

Delmar Johnson lowered the window of his SUV, inhaling as the aromas of damp eucalyptus and wood-smoke wafted in.

He brushed aside the long tendrils of an enthusiastic ivy plant to find the security button outside the gates of the Calvin estate. Calma, a carefully aged metal sign declared. Del had found the place easily, despite the long upward climb along a narrow road etched into the side of the mountain. *Some people call these hills. But just because the Santa Ynez Range starts at sea level doesn't mean these aren't true mountains. And these twisting lanes*

bordered with lush plantings and high walls must conceal sumptuous estates. He'd have preferred seeing the scenery in golden
afternoon sunlight, but even at night—with uplights illuminating
the towering trees—the area was beautiful.

"Yes," squawked the speaker on the ivy-covered wall.

"Deputy Johnson!" announced Del, his voice crashing through
the still night air.

A low hum resonated with the smooth motion of a well-oiled
gate as it swung slowly inward. The driveway then sloped back
down toward the ocean and a Y-intersection came into view with
a sign pointing in each direction. A right arrow indicated *Service
Entrance;* the left arrow was labeled *Main Entrance & Cottages.*
Taking the left, Del stepped on the accelerator to travel the final
quarter-mile around and down to the level site of the main house.

*This must be it . . . a circular driveway in front of the entrance.
Old California they call this. Built in the style of the Santa Barbara
Mission.*

He noticed that the driveway continued onward, apparently
toward the cottages—whoever used them. But he parked at the
main house and crunched across gravel, then walked up the three
wide steps. By the illumination of wrought-iron wall sconces on
either side of the entrance, he took in the details of the heavy
carved oak front door and its seasonal dcor, an elaborate pine
wreath festooned with gilded cones and shiny red berries. *Real,
or fake?* Just as Del's hand reached up to touch the wreath, the
door opened abruptly, and he yanked his arm back to his side.

Del looked into the cool, gray eyes of a handsome, well-
dressed man who stood about his own height of six-foot-two.
*Mid-sixties, fit, self-assured. Silver hair neatly trimmed and perfectly
groomed; tan sweater, probably cashmere; high polish on expensive loafers. Must be Joseph Calvin.*

"Good evening, Detective." The man looked past Del into the
dark. "Weren't there supposed to be two of you?"

"I'm afraid Detective Dexter has been detained and won't be
able to get here in time. I'm Deputy Johnson."

"I see. Come in. I'm Joseph Calvin, by the way." He paused in the doorway only long enough to let Del enter, then spun on his heel, leaving Del to close the front door. As Calvin led the way into his home, the footsteps of the two men echoed on terra cotta tile, the sounds rising through the high atrium of the central stairway. Del's nostrils flared at the spicy scent of cut lilies that perfumed the chill air from their perch on a foyer table.

As they entered a spacious room lined with bookshelves, Mr. Calvin began, "I appreciate your meeting me this late. I thought we'd talk here in my library. Please have a seat. My butler has the night off, but I'll go get us some mineral water. Please make yourself comfortable. I'll be right back."

Before sitting, Del took the moment to take in the hand-wrought elegance of the home—what he could see of it. *I've only seen a home like this in photographs at the library. It's obvious nothing in here is mass-produced. The exterior is the traditional Spanish style of El Pueblo Viejo, like the County Courthouse and the Lobero Theatre with paseos, courtyards, cornices. And inside, these open spaces, but with alcoves tucked into corners; that arched hallway leading off from the foyer, maybe to the kitchen, but who knows? And I think this fireplace is made from cantera stone.* Though massive, it sent forth a glow that warmed the room and gleamed softly on the oversized mahogany desk.

Del walked toward the desk and, before sitting as Calvin had suggested, he angled one of the carved chairs so his back wouldn't face the door.

Calvin returned, walked to the far side of his desk and placed a tray with two bottles of designer sparkling water. "Hope you don't mind drinking from the bottles."

"No, not at all." *Interesting way to start this . . . with the master of the mansion serving me.* Del twisted the cap off the cold glass container, listening to the hiss of escaping gas. "Appreciate it."

Calvin, now seated in his high-backed leather swivel chair, said, "I . . . I really don't know how much I can tell you, but I want you to know I take this matter very seriously. Chris—Ms. Christian—is a friend of mine. I'm worried about her."

"I see." As Del shifted his weight to reach into the inside breast pocket for his notebook, his leather belt creaked. He adjusted the belt, wincing as his keys and cell phone case scraped against the beautiful chair. Before he could stop himself, Del glanced up at his host, realizing he must look as guilty as he felt. *Last thing I need to do is damage the man's property.* "Sorry if I—"

"Not a problem," Calvin interrupted.

The two men sat in silence for a moment, sipping their drinks. Aware that Calvin was likely taking his measure, Del did the same, using his police training to keep his face neutral. Calvin's expression seemed to him tightly controlled. *A hard man . . . in his own way maybe as hard a man as any I've collared and cuffed. How will he respond if I don't begin the interview?*

Calvin looked at him. "So, shall we get started?"

"If you don't mind." *Doesn't seem uncomfortable even though we're alone . . . or with my being just a deputy . . . or even with my being black.*

Calvin lounged back in his deep library chair, his demeanor suddenly more relaxed, and gave Del an expectant look.

"You last saw Ms. Christian exactly when, Mr. Calvin?" Del held his pen poised over a blank page in his blank notebook, moving it the moment the man spoke.

"It's been a while now . . . seven weeks or so." Calvin shifted position in his chair and crossed his legs.

"Seven weeks? You must've known she was missing. You didn't worry till now?"

"She travels a lot. Overseas, for example. Some of her stories are shot in Asia, some in Europe. She keeps me posted, usually. She was leaving on a trip, going to San Francisco, then to Tokyo. She missed our last appointment, but her plans could sometimes change suddenly. I figured she'd get in touch with me when she wanted to."

"And where did your last encounter take place?" Del looked up from his spiral pad, catching a wistful look on Calvin's face. *The man does seem to have genuine affection for the missing woman.*

"It wasn't an encounter, Deputy. It was a date. She, uh . . . we met at her place in Santa Maria. She'd invited me over—she was working late . . . I didn't get there till about eleven. We'd both been too tired to, uh . . . for any sort of entertainment that night. We simply went to sleep. We both had early appointments the following morning."

"And you left on friendly terms?" Del used the flat tones of a practiced professional, insinuating nothing into his question.

Calvin recrossed his legs and cleared his throat. "Yes, very friendly. We, uh, we were intimate that morning. Although we were interrupted."

Del looked up. "By what, sir?"

"A phone call. *Again!*" Calvin looked out the window into the dark, his brows knitting into a deep furrow.

"You find these calls she receives . . . irritating?"

"She doesn't have good boundaries. Be nice if she could turn the damn machine off once in a blue moon."

Now there's heat in the man's voice, color rising up his neck. "Did you have an argument?"

"A disagreement," Calvin admitted, "even though she didn't pick up." He paused. "But she did listen to a voice message. I over-heard it. That call altered her mood."

"So . . . Ms. Christian has some kind of voice messaging? There was no answering machine in the preliminary report." Del's mind leaped forward. *Is the message still there? Does anyone else have access? Could they have erased it?*

"Yes, yes, she's a journalist, of course she has an answering machine. She often tucks it out of sight. But she never turns the blasted thing off. Drives me crazy." Calvin's voice dropped, choked off by the anxiety that seemed to rise by the minute.

Del edged forward in his chair. "Mr. Calvin, to your knowl-edge, did Ms. Christian erase that message?"

"Not while I was there." Calvin composed himself, uncrossed his legs. "We both dressed in a hurry after that," he continued. "She seemed distracted, rushed. I had an early business meeting. We made another date—a make-up date, we called it . . . literally, in this case—for that very evening, before she was due to take her trip. That morning we had a quick bite—toast and coffee, I think—then left immediately. I opened her car door for her in the parking garage—and watched her drive away before doing the same myself." He paused again. "I never saw or heard from her again."

"What was in the message you overheard?"

"It's been a while now. I don't recall the details. But it was a man's voice saying something about a time frame having changed, and that she had to go to some house if she wanted the story."

"Perhaps we should start there, sir."

"I'm sorry, where, Deputy?"

"The last place you were with Ms. Christian. At her residence."

Joseph leaned forward in his high-backed desk chair. "I . . . it'd be terribly odd being there without her—"

"Her permission? I think she'd want your help, don't you?"

Calvin sighed. "I do. Yes."

"In that case, could we make an appointment sometime this week to meet at her apartment? Seeing it again might spark a suppressed memory. You might notice something missing that we wouldn't be aware of. And you could show us where she keeps the answering machine. Could prove helpful to our investigation." *Best to get a commitment from him right now.* "What day would work for you?"

Calvin glanced toward the dark window again and, as though reading his calendar on the pane, he said, "Today's Wednesday. Friday's no good, because we have a big party here that evening and I have to be here all day." Turning to Del, he continued, "I think tomorrow afternoon would work, Deputy. Call my secretary to confirm the time."

"I'll do that. And I'll clear this with Detective Dexter, see if he can come with us, or meet us there."

"Either way, Deputy. It's also fine if it's just you and me at Chris's home."

Del nodded. "All right. In any case, I'll call you to confirm, Mr. Calvin." Del put away his notebook, finished his water, and stood. "The department will appreciate your cooperation."

Calvin saw him to the front door, and as it closed behind him, Del saw the rain had turned to a light drizzle that misted the grounds. He glanced at the circular drive, its exits marked by illuminated end posts. Each lantern seemed to hover, framed by a ghostly rainbow, the particulates of moisture that still hung in the air acting as tiny prisms. *And that's how a case gets solved . . . each clue acting like a lens.*

He inhaled again the pungent aroma from the eucalyptus trees laced with smoke from Calvin's fireplace. *The missing woman probably stood right here, inhaling this same fragrance, enjoying time here with Joseph Calvin.*

Calvin's connection to her . . . the fact that he's now revealed more than we knew. . . . It opens up a whole new avenue of inquiry, gives us something solid. Maybe we can find Christine Christian.

Light shot through the kaleidoscope in her consciousness and made a new geometry of her soul. When had colors been so vivid . . . complexity of design so pure?

Yet even as she yearned to touch it, flow through its matrix, lose herself to the rainbow of light and become its prism, something tugged at the edges of memory.

Christine. *It seemed a nice name—a familiar one. Pristine Christine . . . a childhood song echoed but she regarded the taunt as though from a great distance.*

Now an urgency began to press like a weight against her chest. A few moments ago—or was it a few weeks?—she'd wanted to breathe. Now that seemed irrelevant.

But something else prodded insistently. Yes, there it was—the need to tell.

She remembered now. The story—she had a story to tell, but she didn't have all the details yet. She'd tried to write it. But first there was more research to be done.

The details began to come back into focus, and with them the anxiety increased. What had she done wrong? She'd been smart, diligent, kept her priorities: delayed her dinner date, gone to the house on the bluff to follow the lead, meet her source.

The reporter's instinct that still pulsed within her said danger was still coming closer. That story was the urgency pulling at her, dragging her back to the human circumstances, holding her in the dark. She had to get this story done in time.

Deadline.

The word carried with it the weight of the world.

Prologue

Senior Deputy Delmar Johnson had a date with a ghost. No matter how many times he denied the absurd notion, some unmistakable presence seemed to haunt him.

Nervously, he glanced at the empty chair across the table from where he sat in the restaurant. A shiver ran down his spine. *Does it matter if my date is no longer among the living?*

He shook his head as though to clear away the tendrils of an eerie dream and force his mind into its usual, methodical approach to his cases. Though broadcast journalist Christine Christian's body had never turned up, a gnawing intuition told him the missing woman would not be found alive.

He'd made special arrangements with the missing reporter's former television station to gain access to her most recent broadcast tapes. Whatever stories she'd been working on at the time might provide some clues to her disappearance. At the very least, he'd get a sense of who she was. He'd picked up the tapes himself from KOST-TV, and they had to be returned in a timely fashion.

But not before he gave them a thorough viewing. *Tonight's the night.*

Technically, he shouldn't be racking up overtime on a Sunday, but when a case wouldn't let him alone, he often found the best time to work was into the wee hours, when phones didn't ring and colleagues didn't interrupt. He justified his marginal breach of protocol by reassuring himself he was up to speed on all his other cases.

About a recent reprimand, however, he couldn't let himself off the hook so easily. Under orders from his supervisor Detective Rogers, Delmar had interviewed Mr. Joseph Calvin three months earlier. Calvin had been a friend of Ms. Christian, eventually concerned about her unexplained absence. Del had conducted the interview at Calvin's estate in Santa Barbara, but then also met Calvin in Santa Maria, allowing him to enter the premises of Chris Christian's condo. This, apparently, had been deemed inappropriate. And though nothing official had been inserted in Del's personnel jacket, the verbal admonition still stung.

Perhaps to distract himself—or maybe just to give himself something pleasant to offset the sour residue of the professional slap—Del had decided to have an early dinner at the Lighthouse Tavern. He'd only heard about it since moving here, but had no firsthand experience.

There were several real lighthouses on the Central Coast: Point Hueneme at Oxnard; Point Conception in Santa Barbara; Point San Luis in Avila Beach, all to the south, and Point Sur near Monterey farther north. Between them stood the Piedras Blancas light just north of Milford-Haven—the closest local lighthouse, now automated and inaccessible to visitors.

He'd been curious as to why Milford-Haven had only this pseudo-light . . . realistic enough to fool the eye, but without the powerful beam that would be visible from the sea. So, after a long morning run and a session at the gym down in Morro Bay, he'd gone home to shower, shave and dress in some pressed chinos and a brown blazer. Then, out of uniform for once, he'd driven to the Tavern to introduce himself.

As he'd pulled into the parking lot, he'd been unsure whether he'd find a tourist trap or a quaint coastal gem. As it turned out, he liked the place, and its owner. Michael Owen looked him straight in the eye when he talked, and seemed devoted to the culinary craft, sharing details of the special he was preparing for this evening's menu. Owen was also apparently a successful businessman, as his restaurant had the reputation of drawing both tourists and locals.

Del ordered fish-and-chips—apparently a regular item here, and favorite of his. Sipping something cold at the bar that offered a view into the kitchen, so Del took one of the comfortable high stools. After ordering, he asked about the history of the building, wondering why what appeared to be a real lighthouse was not being used as such.

Michael delivered Del's drink and, rag in hand, automatically wiped down the gleaming bar. Then, picking a clean, dry cloth, he began polishing a glass. "Odd thing is, there are actually two 'unreal' lighthouses here in Milford-Haven."

"Is that right?" Del asked, taking a sip of the plain soda and lime he'd ordered. He might occasionally have a beer at home, but he never drank and drove, and never drank alcohol while on call—which was pretty much always, given his job.

"Well, this one's not really a fake. It's real enough. Just never got commissioned."

According to the story Michael recounted, if Aberthol Sayer —an entrepreneur from Milford Haven, Wales in the 1880s— had succeeded with his ambitious plan, the American Milford-Haven would've had its own lighthouse.

Sayer had moved to California in 1875, the successful owner of a small shipping firm. Taking stock of developments on the Central Coast, he couldn't help but notice what a bustling export center the Piedras peninsula had become for the region. Convinced that Milford-Haven's smaller point of land slightly farther south posed a treacherous obstacle for fishermen, Sayer had believed that by having its own light, the area could develop a profitable fishing industry. He'd thus gone to the trouble and expense of having a defunct lighthouse on the coast of Wales dismantled and transported on one of his ships across the Atlantic, then cross-country by rail from New York to California.

Certain he'd receive the appropriate commission from the U.S. Lighthouse Board, which had been established in 1852, he'd reassembled the structure at Milford-Haven. He even had his public relations slogan ready to use: "The first lighthouse to shine on two oceans." But because he failed to receive the requisite approval, he was never allowed to install a working Fresnel in the tower. He did install a lesser light . . . but nothing bright enough to "confuse navigation," as the Board had admonished.

"So when you took it over, you converted it into the Tavern?" Del asked.

"Yup. Big job. This adjacent building is the restaurant. Next door on the actual lighthouse ground floor, we have a mini-museum shop. T-shirts, mugs, keychains, that sort of thing. We've got an office up on the next floor, up the spiral stairs. Then a small sleeping room above that, which comes in handy sometimes. Nothing much above that except the light itself—a replica that doesn't put out a seaworthy signal. I mean, it's blacked out on the ocean side, per Coast Guard regulations. But it casts a short beam toward land so our customers can find us."

"Ingenious," Del said. "And, obviously, successful."

"Touch wood," Michael replied, putting his palm on the gleaming wooden bar.

"So where's this other fake located?"

"Farther north, toward San Simeon. But it's deserted."

"Oh, okay, that's what I've glimpsed in passing. If the building's unused, I guess it's always dark," Del surmised.

"Right. It's hard to see because it's on private land, way out on a promontory, where it's lower than Highway 1 and shrouded by the coastal pines that've grown much taller since the building was first erected."

"Who owns it?" Del inquired.

"A trust, left by the owners. There've been rumors of a resort going in."

"That would make a big change, shift the character of things in Milford-Haven," Del remarked.

"Yeah, but every time *that* notion rears its ugly head, the town fathers and mothers go nuts. Not really a worry, though. The trust wouldn't allow it."

Del took a sip of his soda. "Ever been inside?"

"Naw. I don't know anyone who has. Heard a lot of stories, though," Michael admitted. "Damnedest thing. Don't know why they built it. I mean, from what I understand, it's just a look-alike shell."

"At a glance, pretty realistic," Del commented.

"From the outside, yeah," Michael agreed. "The original owners built it back in the 1950s."

"Looks like it's attached to a mansion. Must have a cost a fortune, even then."

Michael laughed. "Yeah. Well, nothing on the level of the Hearst property farther north."

"The Hearst Castle? No, I guess not."

"Still," Michael went on, "the owners were a wealthy couple, private almost to the point of secrecy. They had traveled, collected treasures, and this was what they built to enjoy it all, so they say."

"I guess if you have that kind of money, you can do whatever you like," Del reflected. "What were their names?"

"Well, it was something like Joan."

"No, I meant the last name," Del clarified.

"Yeah, that is the last name. I mean, I never saw it written down, just heard stories. 'J' pronounced 'Y.'"

"Hispanic?" Del asked.

"Naw. Welsh, is what I heard."

"Welsh? Hmm, not familiar. Might be fun to research."

"If you like that sort of thing," Michael said, finishing with the glassware.

A waiter delivered Del's plate—crisp, piping hot, lightly breaded fish, french fries, coleslaw, and a big wedge of lemon. "Man, this looks great," he said, salivating while he slipped the napkin onto his lap.

"Good, good," the restauranteur said. "Whatever happens to that old estate, I hope it stays private, and never becomes some huge tourist thing. People move here to get away from that kind of thing, you know? We all need to make a living, but we like it peaceful."

"I hear that," Del agreed.

"Enjoy!" Michael exhorted, leaving his customer to his meal. Del sank his teeth into his first bite, savoring the fresh flavor. As he continued to relish his meal, he thought further about the moribund old lighthouse. He imagined it was only a matter of time before someone bought it. Perhaps it'd be a creative type, since Milford-Haven was full of artists and "makers" of all kinds. But for now, some forty-plus years later, the lighthouse stood quietly in the shadow of trees and rugged coastline, apparently content to remain concealed and keep its secrets, whatever they might be.

As he waited for his check after an excellent meal, Del took a final sip of coffee and pressed the napkin to his lips. He turned his gaze toward the restaurant's window to marvel again at the view—a sweep of coastal scenery that would have few equals . . . all the more spectacular at close of day, with sunset painting vivid streaks across low-hanging clouds.

After paying his bill and thanking Michael again, Del stepped outside into the March evening. The sun had sunk into the water, the sky overhead just beginning to deepen to a Prussian blue. *Nice the days aren't quite as short as they were a few weeks ago.*

The signs of early spring were everywhere on the Central Coast. Rains were no longer the steady pummelings of winter, but had shifted to blustery, intermittent storms. Tiny buds dotted the deciduous trees, and just yesterday he'd seen rows of huge ice-plant flowers blooming along the beach at the Cove. Now a faint trace of jasmine hung in the air like the perfume of a woman who'd passed by and disappeared. *Ironic that in this season of renewal, the life of a young woman has almost certainly been cut short.*

Cast of Characters

Joseph Calvin: mid-60s, 6′1, gray eyes, steel-gray hair, clean-shaven, lean, handsome; CEO of Santa Barbara's Calvin Oil; eligible widower; dates several women including Christine Christian.

Christine Christian: early-40s, 5′6, aqua eyes, blonde, vivacious, beautiful, intense; special investigative reporter for Satellite-News TV station KOST-SATV; lives in Santa Maria; frequent international traveler; dates Joseph Calvin.

Kuyama Freeland: mid-70s, 5′7, pale gray eyes, long white hair down her back, strong and graceful, unadorned, Native American, a Chumash Elder.

Deputy Delmar Johnson: early 40s, 6′2, brown eyes, black hair, handsome, muscular, African-American; with the San Luis Obispo County Sheriff's Department, assigned to the Special Problems Unit; originally from South Central Los Angeles.

Miranda Jones: early 30s, 5′9, green eyes, long brunette hair, beautiful, lean, athletic; fine artist specializing in watercolors, acrylics and murals; a staunch environmentalist whose paintings often depict endangered species; has escaped her wealthy Bay-Area family to create a new life in Milford-Haven.

Mr. Man: age unknown, dark eyes and hair, medium height, medium build; one of reporter Chris Christian's anonymous sources.

Emily Wilkins: late 30s, 5′6, brown eyes, blond hair, Attractive and focused, soft-spoken but determined. Originally from South Africa, where her journalism career hit a stone wall with Apartheid, she moved to Milford-Haven and loves her new home as local journalist.

Milford-Haven Recipes

Dill & Goat Cheese Omelette

(As prepared by Chris Christian from fridge & freezer staples)

Serves 1

Ingredients:
- 2 fresh eggs
- 1 T. Dill, fresh or dried
- 1 T. Shallots, fresh or dried
- 1 T. Butter
- salt and pepper to taste

Directions:
1. Melt butter in small skillet.

2. Saute shallots until just turning golden.

3. Stir in dill, continue to saute lightly. Set aside savory mixture.

4. Beat eggs till frothy, swirl into pan. Continue to swirl the pan occasionally as the edges of the egg begin to set.

5. Reduce heat, cook eggs for another minute, then add savory mixture and goat cheese to omelette center.

6. Cook one more minute, then fold omelette over, and serve.

*Provided by Mara Purl

Milford-Haven Recipes

Lobster Mac & Cheese

(As heated up by Delmar Johnson,
from Linn's Restaurant in Cambria)

Linn's enclave of restaurants, cafes and shops are an institution in Cambria. John and Renee were among the very first sponsors of *Milford-Haven,* when it first aired on KOTR in Cambria.

Their son Aaron has helped with catering *Milford-Haven* gatherings over the years, and has hosted many meals for us. And the **A La Carte Boutique & Books** sells the Milford-Haven Novels.

If you visit the Central Coast, be sure to stop by for a meal, some shopping, and to take home some frozen or packaged jams, pies, or other goodies!

If you love great Mac 'n Cheese, order it from the restaurant then take it home to eat right away, or freeze it to have on hand.

www.LinnsFruitBin.com

Mac'n Cheese by Linn's Restaurant

COLOPHON

The print version of this book is set in the Cambria font, released in 2004 by Microsoft, as a formal, solid font to be equally readable in print and on screens. It was designed by Jelle Bosma, Steve Matteson, and Robin Nicholas.

The name Cambria is the classical name for Wales, the Latin form of the Welsh name for Wales, Cymru. The etymology of *Cymru* is *combrog*, meaning "compatriot."

The California town of Cambria is named for its resemblance to the south-western coast of Wales, where the town of Milford Haven has existed since before ancient Roman times, and is mentioned in William Shakespeare's *Cymbeline*.

The dingbat is the Sand Dollar, drawn by artist Mary Helsaple, and rendered graphically by cover designer Rebecca Finkel. The sand dollar is an irregular echinoid whose surface has a pattern resembling five petals, with five sets of tube feet used for respiration. With a color of purple, brown, yellow, green or black while alive, once dead the test, or endoskeleton, is white, and may appear silver on sand, giving it the appearance of a silver dollar. The sand dollar is a Christian symbol of Christ's birth, death and resurrection, and a Chumash symbol for the progress of the soul into spirit.

LIGHTHOUSE

Each of the *Milford-Haven Novels & Novellas* features a real light-house. In the case of this paranormal tale, four California lighthouses are visited.

The first, also featured in What the Heart Knows is the Piedras Blancas lighthouse located north of San Simeon and nearest the fictional town of Milford-Haven.

The second, also featured in *Where the Heart Lives,* is the Point Vicente lighthouse in the Palos Verdes neighborhood of Los Angeles.

The fourth, which is depicted at night in the cover art for this book, and which is also featured in *Why Hearts Keep Secrets,* is the Point Conception Lighthouse near Santa Barbara.

The third is the Point San Luis lighthouse which this year cele-brates its 130th anniversary. Located above beautiful San Luis Bay and adjacent to delightful Avila Beach, the Victorian structure is the only remaining lighthouse of its style in California. The functioning light, still maintained by the Coast Guard, is part of a historic site that can be visited for wonderful tours by making reservations at the light-house website PointSanLuisLighthouse.org.

This lighthouse is the only one on California's Central Coast that hosts special seasonal events open to the public, as well as private events. Mara Purl has plans to host a special Milford-Haven at this lighthouse.

Secret of the Shells

Special Messages about a Woman and Her Self, and about Discovering the Next Chapter . . . of Her Life

 Shell - Sand Dollar: *What the Soul Suspects*

- This "shell" is actually the endoskeleton of a creature in the sea-star family.

- How important do you consider symbols? Do you watch for "signs" and try to interpret what they mean for your own guidance?

- How would you handle an issue of temporary memory loss? Would you seek medical help? Would you seek spiritual help? Would you turn toward your own intuition?

- Would you, like Chris, tend to ignore internal warnings not to go to a dangerous meeting, if it meant something important for your job?

- Have you ever found a place that gave you a great sense of peace and respite? Would you schedule time there on a regular basis? Would it be more valuable to you to visit a quiet place, or an exciting place?

- How important is your legacy? Have you written a will? Do you have specific projects you intend to complete during your life? Do you have plans to teach special skills to others? Are you creating special keepsakes for your inheritors? Will you plan your memorial service?

- Create a hypothetical plan for a soul-restoring vacation you've always wanted to take. Include all the details you can think of including funds, logistics, activities, friends, goals, and so forth. Use this as a Vision Document and track what happens once you have created it.

To discover more about the Secrets of the Shells
visit www.MaraPurl.com.
To reach the author, by e-mail: MaraPurl@MaraPurl.com.
by mail: Mara Purl c/o Milford-Haven Enterprises
PO Box 7304-629
North Hollywood, CA 91603

What the Soul Suspects
Reading Group Topics for Discussion

1. The novels, novellas and novelettes in this series mostly tell a realistic story about life in a small town. But this is a paranormal story. What makes it different? Could you stay with Chris Christian as she tried to understand why she feels out of sorts? She had a head injury, which might have been a mishap, an accident, or a murder. Which do you think it was?

2. Though several books in the series take place in Milford-Haven, this book takes place in several Central Coast locations. Did you find it interesting to learn more about the entire region?

3. The story focuses on Christine Christian, a successful journalist. She began her career as a newspaper reporter in New York. A few years later a job offer took her to Los Angeles, and then she became a top broadcast journalist in the Central Coast. Do you consider journalism to be a valuable profession? How do you distinguish between authentic news and "fake news"?

4. Deputy Delmar Johnson is pragmatic and rigorous in his approach to solving crimes. But others in his family have a "Gift." Was Del right to doubt their experiences? Do you think he successfully balances his intuition with his professional findings?

5. This novella has an unusual timeline, where Delmar is experiencing "real time" while Chris has come unstuck from time and travels to places guided by a series of insights, or lessons. Do you find this plausible?

6. In addition to being a performer, Mara Purl also spent several years working as a professional journalist. Do you feel her understanding of research and writing makes her writing more realistic?

7. Why is this book called What the Soul Suspects? Do you believe Chris or Delmar learned a lesson about intuition? Do you believe in the spiritual guidance they each experience in this book?

To share or print these discussion points please visit:
http://marapurl.com/books/what-the-soul-suspects

Mara Purl, author of the popular and critically acclaimed *Milford-Haven Novels,* pioneered small-town fiction for women.

Mara's beloved fictitious town has been delighting audiences since 1992, when it first appeared as *Milford-Haven, U.S.A.*©—the first American radio drama ever licensed and broadcast by the BBC. The show reached an audience of 4.5 million listeners in the U.K. In the U.S., it was the 1994 Finalist for the New York Festivals World's Best Radio Programs.

Mara was named the Top Female Author for Fiction by The Authors Show, and to date, her books have won more than forty book awards including the American Fiction, Benjamin Franklin, National Indie Excellence, USA Book News Best Books, and Fore-Word Books of the Year.

Mara's other writing credits include plays, screenplays, scripts for *Guiding Light,* cover stories for *Rolling Stone,* staff writing with the *Financial Times (of London),* and the Associated Press. She is the co-author (with Erin Gray) of *Act Right: A Manual for the On-Camera Actor.*

As an actress, Mara was "Darla Cook" on *Days Of Our Lives.* For the one-woman show *Mary Shelley: In Her Own Words—* which Mara performs and co-wrote (with Sydney Swire)—she earned a Peak Award, she has co-starred in multiple productions of *Sea Marks,* and plays the title role in *Becoming Julia Morgan.* She was named one of twelve Women of the Year by the Los Angeles County Commission for Women.

Mara is married to Dr. Larry Norfleet and lives in Los Angeles, and in Colorado Springs.

Visit her website at www.MaraPurl.com where you can subscribe to her newsletter and link to her social media sites. www.MaraPurl.WordPress.com. She welcomes e-mail from readers at MaraPurl@MaraPurl.com.

MARA PURL
Milford-Haven

Find Saga Chronology at MaraPurl.com/Books